"This is going to be slow," Brian insisted

He stared down into Beth's face and continued, "I swore, if I ever got the chance to make love to you, I'd show some self-control. But I don't know what happens when I'm with you...."

His gaze traveled across her breasts. "Yes, I do," he murmured roughly, lowering his head.

It was Beth who feared losing control when Brian left her quivering breasts to kiss his way down her body. She gasped in pleasure as his lips adored her, tormented her.

She'd die if she didn't have him that very instant. "Brian," she protested, "it would be perfect now. It couldn't get any more perfect."

"Oh, yes, it could," he maintained and proceeded to demonstrate.

Janet Bieber and **Joyce Thies** have once again joined forces, writing as Jenna Lee Joyce. The result? *Awake unto Me*, a unique love story that will stir all your emotions. We're sure this book will become one of your favorite Temptations.

Because readers are so special to them, Janet and Joyce want to extend a special message to all of you: "May this, the most beautiful of seasons, bring you and yours the warmest of memories and the happiest of moments." Cheers!

Books by Jenna Lee Joyce

HARLEQUIN TEMPTATION

These books may be available at your local bookseller.

Don't miss any of our special offers. Write to us at the following address for information on our newest releases.

Harlequin Reader Service
901 Fuhrmann Blvd., P.O. Box 1397, Buffalo, NY 14240
Canadian address: P.O. Box 603,
Fort Erie, Ont. L2A 5X3

Awake unto Me

JENNA LEE JOYCE

Harlequin Books

TORONTO • NEW YORK • LONDON
AMSTERDAM • PARIS • SYDNEY • HAMBURG
STOCKHOLM • ATHENS • TOKYO • MILAN

Dedicated to all the very special people—
doctors, physiotherapists, nurses among them—
who have dedicated their lives to the
neurologically impaired.

Published December 1986

ISBN 0-373-25234-X

1

"ARE YOU READY to get started, Brian?"

Blink.

Beth Crosby ignored her patient's negative response, her bright smile never wavering as she began her morning routine. "C'mon, cowboy. You're going to need all those gorgeous muscles of yours when you come out of this." She lifted Brian's arm off the mattress. "I know you don't think this is doing any good, but it is. I promise."

Beth didn't look at the handsome face against the bed pillow, knowing what she'd see in his eyes. Brian Hadley Towers III had heard too many promises over the past five years and no longer believed any of them. She, on the other hand, had hopes that one day soon he was going to respond to the constant stimuli and snap out of his locked-in state.

She could only imagine what it was like to be able to see and hear, to be aware of everything, yet unable to speak or move. Brian was a prisoner of his own body. The frustration she felt for him couldn't even come close to the kind of frustration he must feel every minute of every day.

"Together we're going to lick this thing," she declared firmly as she rotated his wrist, then took his lifeless hand in both of hers to work the joints of each finger. "This afternoon I'd like to try something different. Electrical stimulation. These range-of-motion exercises keep your muscles functional, but we also want them to be strong. I know how frustrated you are by all this, but tell yourself you're in training. Your football coach wouldn't let up on you until you'd given your best and I'm not going to, either."

Blink.

Blink.

Blink.

No, no, no, Brian repeated, but his physical therapist wasn't looking at him. He could feel the rage working inside him, but the only outlet he had for the emotion was his eyes. Deep crystalline blue, they burned with his frustration while the tall, willowy brunette went blithely on with her work. Why couldn't she leave him alone for just one day? Didn't she realize what her nearness was doing to him?

Beth was twenty-five, the same age as he, but she was so energetic, so full of life. He was as lifeless as a corpse. Unlike the desperation and defeat reflected in his eyes, her large hazel ones sparkled with warmth and enthusiasm. He knew every nuance of their expression. Normally shaded toffee brown, they flashed green when she was angry and glinted gold when she was happy or particularly adamant about something.

Watching her smile was like feeling the heated brilliance of the sun. Her soft, generous lips would open to reveal perfect white teeth and touch off the dainty dimple in her left cheek. Brian hated her when she smiled and hated himself when she didn't.

The sight of her was a constant torment to him, her long supple legs, tiny waist and full breasts a source of unending torture. He longed to run his fingers through the thick mane of her multicolored hair, release the brown, gold and shimmering auburn strands from that damned ponytail she always wore. He'd like to . . .

Blink.

No! He had to stop thinking about all the things he'd like to do to her, with her. It was just that she was so damned beautiful, a constant reminder of all he could never have, of feelings he didn't want to feel but did.

He knew he'd never have her, and that realization was paralyzing his soul, just as the accident had paralyzed everything else. He wanted to scream at her, curse her for touching him when he couldn't respond to her touching, smiling at him when he couldn't return her smile.

Six months! He'd endured her soft hands on his body for six long months. How much longer could he stand it?

"How's our boy today?" Glenda Towers, a petite, delicate-looking woman in her late forties, inquired with forced gaiety as she walked briskly into the room. "Is he ready for another crack at Economics 301?"

I'm a man, Mom, not a boy. And why don't you ask me that question instead of Beth? Brian could almost hear the angry words take form on his lips, but of course they hadn't and never would.

"Why don't you ask him?" Beth had no trouble taking the words out of Brian's immobile mouth. There wasn't any anger in her question, though, only commendable patience.

Glenda apologized for her insensitivity; blue eyes the same color as Brian's conveyed her remorse. Sitting down on the bed, she took her son's limp hand in her own. "What do you say, Brian? Can you listen to Professor Fisher's lecture while Beth works on your legs?"

Blink. *I can't do anything while Beth's working on my legs except think about working on her.*

"Please, Brian. For me?" his mother coaxed. "If we don't keep at this, you'll lose so much time getting your degree once you're well again."

Blink. Blink. Brian gave in. The affirmative response was the only thing he had left to give this kindhearted woman who had sat at his bedside for days, weeks, months. The grief she endured so stoically was a reflection of all he and his parents had lost in the blink of an eye, or more correctly, the sharp slam of his unprotected head against a linebacker's helmet. Gone were the afternoons of glory when he'd donned the scarlet and gray and played football for Ohio State; gone were his degree in business, his plans to step into the family firm and eventually take over... all gone.

If only he'd tested his chin strap before that play. If only he'd missed that pass. If only he'd gone down with the first hit and not dug in and driven for more yardage. If only he hadn't been so close to the goal line, hadn't wanted the win so badly. If only. . .

From that moment to this, his life had been made up of nothing but "if onlys." If only he'd survive the brain surgery. If only he'd awaken from deep coma. If only he'd come out of his locked-in state.

In less than six months he had cleared the first two hurdles but there had been no further success. He'd overheard his doctor's grim whispered prognosis for his chances and knew the game was as good as lost. "I'm sorry Mr. and Mrs. Towers, but I can give you no reason to hope there'll be any change. There's a ninety-nine percent probability that Brain will remain locked in forever, cognizant of what's going on around him but unable to move or communicate."

So far, forever was almost five years, five years of having the use of nothing but his eyes, five years of useless physical therapy to preserve muscles that would never run for another game-winning score, of listening to meaningless lectures to sharpen a mind that would never be called upon to make a decision.

"Don't look like that, Brian!" Glenda's fingers closed tightly on his hand. "You're going to be fine, darling. Please believe that. With Beth here, it's only a matter of time."

Blink. Blink. *Yes.* Brian gave his mother the answer she wanted. The woman still believed in miracles, and it didn't cost him anything to let her go on hoping for one. He owed her that much, if only for the times in those early days when her loving voice and soothing touch had saved him from the grip of absolute panic.

"Is the volume okay?" Glenda asked as she adjusted the headset over Brian's ears.

Blink. Blink.

"Good." Glenda gave him the thumbs-up sign, then turned away, speaking softly to Beth.

Even through the dry tones of Professor Fisher's lecture, Brian picked up on his mother's words. She often forgot that his hearing and sight were acute even if he couldn't move a muscle. "He seems so depressed today, Beth. You don't think he's giving up, do you?"

Brian frowned, though his face didn't reflect his displeasure. His parents were always whispering to Beth about him, seeking her advice. He hated it. The woman already knew all there was to know about him physically. That was humiliating enough, but she knew other things, as well, such as what kind of student he'd been, how he'd behaved as a kid, how the girls had clamored after him once he'd been named quarterback of his high school football team, how he'd made the cover of *Sports Illustrated* as a Heisman Trophy hopeful.

He had no doubt Beth had been forced to look at his baby pictures and been prompted to make suitably appreciative remarks about his big blue eyes and amazing head of gorgeous golden curls. He could imagine his mother cooing, "He was a golden boy even then. So handsome. Don't you think he's handsome, Beth, dear?"

"No," Beth pronounced with certainty.

Brian shot Beth a startled glance before realizing she wasn't responding to his thoughts but to the question his mother had asked her.

"You and I won't let him give up, Glenda. Isn't that why you followed Dr. Samuel's advice and took Brian out of that nursing home, built this fabulous room and hired me to take over his therapy?"

The older woman's classic features immediately lost their pinched look. "Yes, I did. And you're right. My son is going to walk and talk and laugh again." Unaware that Brian had developed a talent for reading lips, Glenda whispered, "I just wish we could convince Hadley that we're going to succeed. He's lost all heart, I'm afraid."

"We'll just have to have enough patience for both of them, then, won't we?" Beth placed her arm around the woman's shoulders. "Don't worry, Glenda. Between the two of us, neither one of them stands a chance."

"Not one," Glenda affirmed vehemently. Her spirits restored, she marched over to the bed and kissed Brian on the cheek. Lifting one earphone, she announced, "I'll be back to see you later this afternoon. Beth tells me you'll be much too busy for another visit until then. Your father and I have to attend one of those charity affairs sponsored by the Towers Foundation. I detest tuna delight. Aren't you glad you don't have to go?"

Blink. Blink.

"Beth says you're having something much more delectable. And, Brian, I want you to stop shooting daggers at her when she gives you your lunch. It's very bad manners."

That said, she replaced the headset, gave them both a jaunty wave and left the room.

As soon as they were alone, Beth took off Brian's earphones. "It must be hard to take when she talks to you like you're a five-year-old."

Blink. Blink.

Beth laughed. "Then stop acting like one."

Blink.

Beth made a face at him, then formed her fingers into claws. "For that, mister, I'm going to give your legs a double workout."

Brian closed his eyes, counted to ten, then opened them again. It was a sign no one except he and Beth knew about. It encompassed a lot of words, but mainly it said, "You win. I give up."

"One of these days, Towers, we're both going to win, but only if neither one of us gives up. Deal?"

Blink. Blink.

"Does that mean you're not going to kill me with your eyes when I help you swallow the delicious *carbonnades à la flamande* that's on today's menu?"

Blink. *No, I hate stew.*

"Fair enough." Beth grinned cheekily at him, then replaced his earphones. His eyes followed her as she walked to the end of the bed and lifted his foot. She rotated the ankle, massaged the arch, then met his intent gaze. "You're not paying any attention to the good professor, Brian. Now get back to your work and let me get back to mine."

A few minutes later, Beth heard voices in the hall, but she didn't pause in the routine she'd done since the morning after her arrival. She glanced up at Brian and saw that he had his eyes closed. He'd either taken her advice and was concentrating on Professor Fisher's lecture, or he'd fallen asleep. Whichever, he didn't see the tall, silver-haired man who took one step into the room, then quickly retreated. It was just as well.

Beth knew that Brian's accident had been a terrible blow to his parents, but Brian's father had taken it the hardest. Every time Hadley Towers came to visit Brian, Beth could see his disappointment and despair, his regret over the loss of all the dreams that he felt no longer had any chance of coming true. Brian saw it, too, and after each visit, he'd close his eyes, shutting down all communication until he'd controlled the pain. Sometimes it took him hours.

Beth completed Brian's range-of-motion exercises, functional movement patterns and then the thorough massage that followed. As she rubbed a warm, soothing oil into his skin, she had to acknowledge that it was getting harder and harder to maintain her objectivity where he was concerned. Unlike Brian's father or Jake Halloran, Brian's personal attendant, and the few friends that still came to visit him, Beth looked upon Brian as a man, a man who could experience the full range of human emotions but had no way of communicating his feelings.

The more she had learned about him, what he'd been like before his accident, the more obsessed she'd become with the idea that he had to recover. He was so young, so vital, had so much to give. Beth was honest enough to admit that she couldn't bear the thought of his perfect body wasting away to nothing. In her opinion, though, a far greater waste would be the loss of a beautiful mind. Without saying a word, Brian Towers had conveyed his unique intelligence, rare wit and sensitivity. If Beth had anything to say about it, Brian would one day reclaim his rightful place in the world.

She and Brian had formed a very special relationship over the past six months and it went beyond their patient-therapist association. Sometimes Beth would see the desperation in his eyes, be so in tune with his feelings that she'd be able to put his thoughts into words. If she was on target, as she usually was, he would blink yes over and over again. Then she would try her best to convince him that he shouldn't give up hope. At those times they were very close, communicating on a level that didn't require words.

It was Beth's steadfast optimism and determined efforts with patients that had gained her the well-paying job as Brian's live-in therapist and allowed her to put her most unorthodox theories to the test. This was her chance to prove that constant stimulation, mental as well as physical, was the best way to break through the mind block that held people like Brian prisoner in their own bodies, and she was determined to succeed.

Glenda Towers had heard of Beth's reputation and offered her a salary that she would have been a fool not to accept. However, it wasn't the high pay that made Beth decide to take the job. It was the opportunity to devote all her skills to just one patient, a very special patient, who had touched her heart from the very first moment she'd laid eyes on him.

Glenda had provided the best possible working conditions. She had prevailed upon her husband, even though he saw little chance of his son recovering, to have a room built for Brian's physical therapy. The facility surpassed many being used in nursing homes, clinics and public hospitals, which suffered from lack of funds; no expense had been spared on supplies or equipment. Glenda was sure that Brian was going to get well, and her enthusiasm had finally rubbed off on her husband.

Once the convalarium had been built, however, therapy started and months had gone by with no change in his son's condition, Hadley's zeal had gradually died. Now he rarely entered the large, sun-filled addition that housed a circular bed, a stretch chair, a Hoyer lift, a large mat table and a whirlpool bath. As far as he was concerned, all the expensive equipment in the world couldn't give him back his son.

Up to a point Beth had to agree with him. The equipment was important, but it was the round-the-clock care Brian was receiving that might truly make the difference. Even more of a help to Brian was his mother's wholehearted cooperation with Beth's course of treatment. Nothing Beth proposed was ever vetoed if there was the slightest chance it might help Brian.

Besides her training and experience in physical therapy, Beth was also certified in neuro-developmental training and could offer Brian much more than routine care. But beyond that, she absolutely refused to give up on him. She'd been working at the Towers mansion for six months now without achieving any visible results. Still, she wouldn't allow herself the slightest doubt that Brian Hadley Towers III would one day enjoy a normal life.

Twenty minutes later, she and Jake draped Brian's shorts-clad body over the huge leather ball that was used to stretch the muscles of his lower back and keep his spine in proper alignment. Beth sat on the floor and held on to Brian's wrists as Jake rolled the ball from left to right, then backward and forward.

Though Jake rarely had more than two words to say, Beth was extremely grateful for his assistance. Brian was very lean, not an ounce of fat to soften the lines of the long muscles she'd worked so hard to maintain, but he was an inch over six feet tall and still outweighed her by more than sixty pounds. No one outweighed Jake. He was six and a half feet of pure bulging muscle.

To break the silence, Beth inquired, "Did the equipment I ordered arrive?"

Jake nodded.

"Can you set it up right after lunch?"

Another nod.

"I'm really excited about starting this program of electrical stimulation."

"Uh-huh."

Beth sighed and glanced at Brian. Head down, he couldn't see the frustrated expression on her face. Scooting across the floor, Beth ducked her head under Brian's so he could see her. She was sure he knew what she was thinking, so she winked at him before sliding back into position.

Wynkin', Blynkin' and Nod, Brian thought wryly. He'd dubbed them with those names months ago. Of the three of them, Beth was the only one who could complete a sentence. Jake was excruciatingly shy, and he was . . . he was gagged by an insurmountable neurological defect.

As the pain in his arms intensified, he decided Beth deserved to suffer some sort of punishment for all she'd put him through. It was poetic justice that this ceaselessly perky woman who loved to talk had been stuck with two nontalkers. Of course, that didn't stop her from keeping up a steady stream of conversation. If he'd been able, he'd have laughed at the countless times he could recall her talking to herself and answering her own questions.

"Lunchtime," Beth declared brightly when she'd decided Brian had had enough. Although he wasn't aware that his muscles were under any strain, his skin had produced a very healthy sheen of sweat. "Let's get him into the chair, Jake."

Brian closed his eyes. This maneuver always made him feel like an oversized baby. Jake flipped him over on the ball, then lifted him up into his beefy arms as if he weighed nothing. All the while, Beth kept up a non-stop chatter about the next step in a process he'd had memorized after the second day. If he ever got his capabilities back, he was going to tell her that his mother wasn't the only one who sometimes treated him like a five-year-old.

Then again, any self-respecting five-year-old could dress and feed himself. No wonder everyone occasionally forgot that they weren't dealing with a helpless child but a helpless man. In his worst moments of self-pity, he forgot it, too.

Lunch was the ordeal it always was. Beth massaged his lips until they opened wide enough to allow a spoon inside his mouth. Then she stroked his throat until the runny paste she always labeled with some exotic name had trickled down inside. Worse than the humiliation of needing Beth's help even to swallow was his embarrassing reaction to her nearness.

And she was near, very near. She leaned across him to get as close as she could to his mouth and her soft breasts pressed into his chest. Sometimes, like today, she didn't even bother to get him into a shirt or cover him with a drop cloth, and he was treated to the feel of her smooth, tanned arms brushing the hair on his chest. It was obvious she had no idea that his body's frequent reactions to her presence and touch were anything but involuntary. She certainly never acted as if she even noticed. She was in for one hell of a surprise if he ever got the opportunity to tell her about all the sensations he'd experienced while she was manhandling his body.

Beth began using a warm, moist cloth to wipe off the spills on his chest. The slow, circular motions seemed to drive Brian mad and he groaned. Immediately Beth stopped all movement, her lovely features masked with concern. "Are you hurting, Brian?"

Blink. Blink. *I'm hurting all right, you beautiful sadist.*

Beth knew that pain shouldn't necessarily be taken as a sign of returning function, but Brian seemed to be groaning more and more often lately. Did it mean something? "Is it so bad that we should take inventory?"

Blink. *Absolutely not!*

"Taking inventory," as she called it, involved Beth running her hands over every part of him while he blinked yes or no to indicate pain. If she touched him where he was aching right now, she definitely wouldn't like the answer she'd get.

"I'm glad. That means there's no reason we can't start electrical stimulation today."

Blink.

"Hmmm." Beth considered his response, not sure what he was trying to tell her. "Let me put this another way. Is there any reason why you don't want me to try it?"

Blink. Blink. *Because it's going to hurt like hell.* Brian tried to convey that message with his eyes, and Beth, with her usual uncanny instincts where he was concerned, knew exactly what he was trying to say.

"Yes, it's going to hurt, but the pain will be worth it." Her warm hazel eyes were tinged with gold, expressing her seriousness more eloquently than her words could. "Your muscles haven't undergone any really strenuous activity since your accident. While you were playing football you were always in peak condition. You lifted weights and exercised. You pushed yourself, sometimes when it hurt, to build your body."

With a bewitching blink of long lashes, the gold washed away and specks of green splintered in the center of her irises as she chided, "You probably experienced more pain doing some of those things than you will from the little electrode I'm going to poke you with. Just think of electrical stimulation as another kind of workout. Don't you think you owe it to yourself to keep those muscles you spent years developing in the best shape you can?"

Blink. That said, Brian closed his eyes so he couldn't see the gentle rebuke in hers. He hated that particular look because he always gave in to it, and when he gave in, it always meant she'd devised some new torture for him. Little electrode. Hah! It was probably six feet long.

Beth looked at him steadily, refusing to accept his answer. His body couldn't be allowed to atrophy from disuse. It was too beautiful; he was too beautiful.

She loved the shape of his head, the waving blond hair that capped it and softened his rugged features. The dark lashes that hid his marvelous blue eyes were thick, the ends dipped in gold to match his brows. His mouth was firm and very masculine. Everything about him was a sculptor's delight, including his well-defined chin, straight nose and stubborn jaw.

Brian's physique made him every woman's dream of Prince Charming. Even though he was much too thin, he still had the broad shoulders, narrow hips, tight waist and lean buttocks that proclaimed him an attractive male. No, he wasn't the prince, but more like a masculine Sleeping Beauty, just waiting for the touch of a pair of loving lips to bring him back to life.

Just a kiss. Wouldn't it be a miracle if that were all it took? Beth was taken aback by her train of thought. She knew every inch of this man's body, but never before had she allowed herself the luxury of thinking what it would be like to kiss him. But, then, what harm could it do? They were friends, weren't they? It would be a friendly kiss.

She knew fairy tales didn't come true, but . . . No, it was ridiculous to think for even one moment that the touch of her lips would have any effect on him whatsoever. She was being silly, unbelievably fanciful.

Beth placed her hand under Brian's chin, but he still didn't open his eyes. She gave him a playful tap on the nose. No response.

"C'mon Brian. Let's talk about this electrical stimulation business."

Nothing. Beth considered what to do next. Brian was being stubborn, just asking for it. A few seconds later, he got it.

His eyes flew open, registering shock. For the first time in five years, he was feeling a woman's lips on his own. And not just any woman's—Beth's! Beth was kissing him, actually doing what he'd been willing her to do for so long.

After months of careful scrutiny, he'd known that her lips would be soft, but that word didn't come close to describing what they actually felt like. Warm, moist, incredibly feminine and tender. He wanted to cry at the sheer pleasure of it, the relief that he wasn't going to die without ever again having felt the intimate touch a woman gives to a man she cares about.

It was over much too soon and he wanted to scream in frustration.

"That got your attention, huh?" Beth's cheeks were slightly flushed, but her words showed no hint of embarrassment.

Blink. Blink. The signal was given with far more enthusiasm than usual.

Beth laughed, then gave him a quick peck on the cheek. "I'll have to remember this if you ever shut down on me like that again." Then she frowned as it occurred to her that what she had just done could only make Brian yearn for all the tactile pleasures that were presently lost to him. Kissing him had been a cruel reminder, and she wouldn't do it again.

"Electrical stimulation." She held up a warning finger in case he was ready to close her out again. "I just want to tell you about it, okay?"

Blink . . . Blink. No enthusiasm at all.

"Coward," she teased. "It's very simple. I'll touch an electrode to each muscle and a small shock will make it contract. I promise you this procedure is very safe and controlled. I'm not going to injure you, but I won't lie and tell you there isn't going to be pain. There will be, but I want you to concentrate on the benefits."

Blink. Blink.

"Then I've got your okay?" Her eyes lit up with expectation. "The equipment arrived this morning, so we can get started right away."

Blink.

Beth placed her hands on her hips and scowled. "You're so blasted stubborn sometimes."

They stared at each other for several seconds, neither relenting. It was a standoff. They'd had several similar confrontations in the past, but eventually Beth always won.

This time, however, Brian wasn't going to give in. He'd taken quite enough of her abuse. He'd been poked, jabbed, prodded and stretched for the last time.

In a voice hoarse from years of disuse, he croaked, "Lady, the day I let you use a cattle prod on me will be the day I die!"

2

"NOW YOU LISTEN TO ME Brian Towers. Elec—" Beth's mouth dropped open in stunned disbelief. "Brian? Brian, you just talked!"

Brian felt as if a two-ton weight had suddenly been lifted off his face. He could move his lips, his tongue. He could smile!

He knew it was a stupid smile, a drunken, lopsided smile. But it was something. He could feel it. He was responding at will with something other than a damned blink to Beth's comical expression. He'd never seen her at such a loss. She appeared to be paralyzed, frozen in a kneeling position beside his stretch chair.

"Isn't that what you've been working for, Beth?" he asked slowly, his speech somewhat labored.

"Don't move!" Beth ordered in a shaken tone, although she was the one who seemed to have lost all function. She could talk, but her legs absolutely refused to hold her when she tried to stand up. She plopped back down on the floor. "Stay right where you are until I get your parents! Okay?"

"Move?" Brian's expression turned quizzical as he stared down at his arms and legs. Slowly he commanded his fingers to curl into a fist, and they sluggishly responded. His toes. He could wiggle his toes, feel his feet and his legs. He could move everything! "It's over," he whispered. "Oh, God, Beth. It's finally over."

He could feel tears rolling down his cheeks, but when he lifted his hand to brush them away they fell even faster. "D...did you see that? My hand. I...I lifted my hand. And I'm crying. I can cry."

"Oh, Brian." Beth choked the words past the gigantic lump in her throat. Throwing off her professional demeanor, she flung herself forward, wrapped her arms around him and hugged him as tightly as she could. "I'm so happy for you, Brian. So very, very happy."

Brian couldn't tell whose tears were forming a bigger puddle on his chest, his or hers, but it didn't matter. He'd never felt better in his life. Beth was hugging him and he was able to hug her right back. His arms were no longer useless appendages but capable of carrying out the dictates of his brain. Miraculously his functions had been restored and all his senses brought back to strong, pulsating life.

He felt as if he'd been reborn into a world bursting with sensations that he could finally experience to the fullest. For the four and a half years since he'd awakened from a deep coma, he'd been able to hear, see and feel, but none of those senses had been worth anything to him because he couldn't communicate or initiate a response. Now when something hurt he could yell. When something felt good he could say so.

"You feel so good," he breathed softly, rubbing his cheek against hers. One hand crept slowly, hesitantly down her spine, his fingers memorizing each indentation. "I knew you would."

His lips found her temple, began kissing the soft skin along her hairline as his other hand found its way into her hair. His fingers tangled in the thick strands of her ponytail as his palm cupped the back of her head, keeping it in place upon his chest. It felt so right to have her enclosed in his arms—a dream come true.

For a moment, having been so overwhelmed by happiness, Beth had forgotten that she was his therapist, not a member of Brian's immediate family. She shouldn't be the one hearing his first words, accepting his first faltering attempts to reach out to another, or witnessing his beginning movements. And she definitely shouldn't be responding to his touch as if she were in the arms of a long-lost lover, enjoying the feel of his lips against her skin, of her cheek against the curling hair on his chest.

Of course Brian was as overwhelmed as she was, so elated by his return to function he didn't realize what he was doing. The poor man had been starving for all the simple things other people took for granted, hugging, touching, kissing. To him, she could have been anyone just as long as she was human.

"Brian," she murmured gently, but the arms around her didn't loosen their hold. "Brian," she repeated more firmly.

"Beth," he responded, seeming to savor each letter of her name as it rolled effortlessly from his lips.

"Let me up, Brian."

"Huh?" Brian didn't want to relinquish the pleasure of holding her, but swiftly realized that Beth had gone stiff in his arms. "What's wrong?" Reluctantly he dropped his hands away, his eyes searching her face when she quickly pushed herself off him.

"We've kept this wonderful happening a secret long enough. I have to go get your folks and call the doctor."

"My folks aren't home."

Beth sat back on her heels, her face a picture of confusion. "Oh, I'd forgotten." She wished Brian would stop staring at her so closely, so strangely, wished she understood that peculiar half smile on his face.

Her cheeks felt as if they were on fire. That was probably what he was staring at, considering how they'd been conducting themselves over the past few minutes. Surely he didn't suspect that her response to his embrace had rapidly changed from simple joy over his recovery to overwhelmingly sensual pleasure at his touch? That could create some very serious problems in the future.

Finally Beth managed to stand up. She immediately stuffed her hands into her pockets to hide their trembling. "Eh . . . well, maybe I should find Jake and give him the wonderful news."

Brian nodded.

"He'll be so surprised."

He nodded again.

"Brian?"

Beth couldn't help laughing as he then proceeded to mimic both her and his male attendant to perfection.

"Isn't it great about Brian, Jake? Uh-huh. Don't you want to go see him and tell him how happy you are? Uh-huh."

"So he's a man of few words," she admonished. "That doesn't mean he won't be just as thrilled as anybody."

"Uh-huh," Brian agreed. "That show should last about two seconds. Then both of you can help me get ready for Mom and Dad. I know I'm going to be weak at first, but by the time they get home, I want to be on my feet and walking. I can't wait to see their faces."

Beth sighed at the obvious excitement in his voice, hating the knowledge that she was going to have to put a damper on his enthusiasm. "That would be great, Brian, but I'm afraid it's too soon for that to be possible. You may not believe it, but you won't be running any races for a few weeks."

Beth recognized the look in his eyes—the stubborn, implacable blaze of blue that signaled his mind was made up. However, she was somewhat unnerved when the look was matched with a facial expression. Up until a few moments ago, she'd only seen his face in a relaxed state. Now his strong jaw was set, his mouth tight and his brows drawn fiercely together. This was a new Brian, one that was going to be infinitely more difficult to handle.

"First things first, Brian," she stated matter-of-factly. "Weak doesn't describe what you'll feel if you try to stand. Your muscles just won't hold you. You have to remember that they haven't been used in years. You're going to have to be patient until we can get you back into normal condition."

"Patient!" Brian shouted, introducing Beth for the first time to his notoriously quick temper. "What the hell have you been doing for the past six months? Preparing me to lie in bed for the rest of my life? What was all that talk about keeping me in shape? A pack of lies? Damn you! Did I go through all that pain and torture for nothing?"

"Torture?" Beth was taken aback by his anger. "Don't be ridiculous. Nothing I did could have caused enough pain to be described as torture."

"The hell it couldn't!" Brian raged. "I've endured six months of you pulling my arms and legs half out of their sockets, of constant poking and prodding. You've frozen me with ice rubs, burned me in steam baths. And if I hadn't come out of this today, you were going to start electrocuting me. And that's only the physical side. Mental torture is your specialty, lady. Every time I'd groan with pain, you'd tell me it was for my own good. Every time I complained, I felt like a wimp."

"Brian, you're not being fair." Beth tried to keep her voice calm even though he'd done his best to put her on the defensive. "Every one of the things you described is a standard treatment and *was* for your benefit. You might have suffered some discomfort, but no way would I call it torture."

"I'd love to hear what you'd call it if the tables were turned and you'd been the receiver of all that standard treatment." Brian's blue eyes cut into her like shards of

ice and his voice, though still rasping, was thick with
sarcasm. "I'd enjoy doing all the things to you that you
seemed to get such a kick out of doing to me."

Beth bit her lip, unable to quell the hurt rising up inside her. For months she'd done everything she could
think of to help him, to make him well again, and now
that he had broken out of the locked-in state, he was
accusing her of taking pleasure in his helplessness and
suffering. Didn't he realize that the only reason he could
move at all was because of the supposed torture she'd
inflicted?

"I'm sorry you feel that way, Brian," she murmured,
turning away before she said something she'd really be
sorry for. She had to remind herself of all this man had
been through, that she was merely an available recip-
ient of the emotional baggage he'd been carrying inside him for so long. Once he'd rid himself of his stored-
up rage and frustration he'd turn back into the coura-
geous, sensitive and caring man she'd been working
with up until today.

Beth didn't know that during their time together,
Brian had learned how to read her facial expressions
very accurately. When she faced him again, he saw the
sheen of tears in her eyes, the tiny quiver in her lower
lip and the slight ashen hue to her skin. He knew how
badly he'd hurt her. He'd never meant to.... Yes, he had.

"Beth?" he began tentatively. Though unwilling to
apologize for expressing his feelings, he still wanted to
make up for dumping all the years of physical and
emotional agony on the one person whose unwaver-

ing goal had been to make him well again. He was a complete jerk for accusing her of wanting to hurt him. "I'm sorry for losing my temper. I shouldn't have taken my frustration out on you. I know you were only trying to help me."

"I'm sorry I hurt you, Brian," Beth replied after a long pause. She still wasn't in as much control as she'd have liked to be, so she kept her face averted while explaining why she'd failed to recognize the extent of his pain. "None of us knew how much you could feel. Pain is an unconscious response. Some locked-in patients register little or no sensation. Others have full range. It was hard to tell to what degree you were feeling anything."

"With my limited vocabulary it was difficult to elaborate."

Beth glared at him. "Whenever I thought you might be hurting, I stopped and asked you. You never indicated your pain was that intense."

"I do have some pride. I didn't want to come across as a martyr."

"Oh, for heaven's sake, Brian," she flung back in exasperation. "Nobody would ever think you're a martyr, considering all you've been through. And why do you think I took inventory? I'm not psychic!"

"I'll say." Brian laughed, the pleasant rumbling sound startling both of them. As Beth turned back to look at him, he grinned more widely and said, "Ah, yes, inventory. Some day I'll tell you how I benefited from that procedure."

His eyes sparkled brightly, signaling his return to good humor. "The real me has come as quite a shock to you, hasn't it?"

Beth thought about this for several moments before answering. She truly felt she knew Brian better than anyone besides his mother did, but it was apparent he didn't realize how much of himself he'd actually managed to communicate. "I always knew the real you had quite a temper. Your eyes have a very explicit vocabulary, and yes, I have a feeling the next few weeks are going to be a real learning experience for me, especially if you start saying all the nasty things you've been thinking for the past six months."

"We're both going to learn a few new things about each other," he agreed.

"You already know all there is to know about me, Brian," Beth corrected. "What you see is what you get. From now on, you'll be able to talk back, but I'm going to be the same slave driver I've always been. Deal?"

"Deal." His voice went softer, quieter still; his gaze was warm. "I need you, Beth."

For a second, Beth had thought he was going to say something entirely different, something that would have made working with him that much harder. Treating a very alert, reactive, communicative Brian was going to be a real challenge, and not just on a professional level. While he'd been locked in, it had become more and more difficult for Beth to hide her personal reactions to him. Now it might prove impossible.

At first she'd felt somewhat maternal toward him. Lately, those tender, motherly feelings had often given way to a keen awareness of his masculinity. Having either reaction wasn't very professional, but of the two, Beth much preferred the former. Lusting after a patient was strictly taboo.

Of course, it was perfectly natural for him to have developed a strong dependence on her, but she was supposed to maintain her objectivity and see his need for what it was. The emotional attachment he had to her could never be the basis of a healthy, lasting relationship. As drawn to him as she was, she had to keep reminding herself that he was her patient and it was her duty as his therapist to help him progress to the point where she'd be out of a job. He'd come a long way, but he still had a long road ahead of him.

As far as her physical reactions to him were concerned, Brian might have a mature male body, look like one of Michaelangelo's finest creations, but his social development had stopped at age twenty. That made her five years older than him in experience, a gap he might be incapable of breaching. It would be better for both of them if she never contemplated his being anything to her but her patient.

"I'm going to go get Jake and then call Dr. Samuels," Beth decreed briskly. "If the good doctor agrees, when your folks get home this afternoon, you're going to be sitting on a chair in the family room. That will shock them just as much as seeing you walking."

"It will, won't it?" Brian shifted impatiently on the recliner, droplets of sweat appearing on his forehead as he struggled to get up from his semiprone position. "Whether Samuels agrees or not, that's what I'm going to do. Tell Jake to hurry, Beth. I can't wait to get off this damned thing." He grinned sheepishly. "Hard to believe, but I'm a little weaker than I look."

Two hours later, Brian was dressed in a blue knit shirt and a pair of faded jeans he hadn't worn since before his accident. He was slouched in a comfortable recliner chair, his long legs stretched out in front of him. He'd refused to make use of the chair's footrest, saying it reminded him too much of the stretch recliner in his room. To him, it was pure joy to bend his knees and plant his feet on the floor.

Beth sat across from him in a matching chair, trying not to laugh as her impatient patient fought a losing battle against sleep. His lashes kept fluttering over his eyes, but he refused to admit that the limited activity he'd indulged in thus far had taken its toll. Whenever Beth glanced over at him, he'd pretend to be fascinated with an article in the magazine he'd requested. Beth was sure he hadn't read a word.

She was also sure that Brian didn't realize how much he'd just asked of his body. Once Jake had arrived in the therapy room and delivered his four-word speech of congratulations on Brian's recovery, their jubilant patient had started firing orders at a rapid pace. In fifteen minutes flat, Beth had found him the clothes he'd wanted to wear, and Jake had helped him to dress.

He had flatly refused to use the wheelchair, and against all of Beth's protestations, had tried to walk to the south wing. With Jake's support, he'd managed to stand up for about thirty seconds, taken a few rubbery steps, then had to admit that he wasn't going to make it down the hallway on his own steam. Once he'd been installed in the family room in the chair nearest the entryway, he'd talked nonstop for over twenty minutes. In the last half-hour he'd barely said two words.

Beth heard a car turn into the circular drive outside and glanced over at Brian. His blond head was slumped to one side, his eyes were closed and his chin was resting on his chest. He'd lost the battle and was sound asleep. She hesitated for a few seconds, then decided he'd never forgive her if she didn't wake him up before his parents came inside and saw him.

"Brian?"

He didn't so much as flicker an eyelash, so she got up and walked over to him. Asleep in the chair, he looked so young and endearing that it was all Beth could do not to reach down and tousle his hair, or deliver a soft kiss to his forehead. Instead she placed her hand on his shoulder and gave him a gentle shake. "They're home, Brian. Wake up."

Beth felt a stab of worry when he didn't immediately respond, which abated quickly when he growled, "Took them long enough."

She tried not to show her fascination as he stretched the body she knew so well. First his long legs shifted, then his arms and finally his shoulders. Every movement he made seemed miraculous, the greatest miracle being the expression on his handsome face. The eyes might be the mirror of the soul, but they couldn't reflect all the little nuances of expression that speak of personality: the lift of a brow, a smile, a frown.

"How do I look?" Brian struggled to a position that would exhibit his restored mobility. "How's this? Do you think they'll be able to tell that I've come back to the real world?"

"You look great," Beth assured him. "They'll take one look at you and know they've got their son back. You're grinning like a hyena."

If she were Glenda or Hadley Towers, Beth would have grieved most for the loss of Brian's smile. Slightly lopsided, infinitely charming, it was the kind of smile that could melt even the hardest heart. Beth's insides dissolved into warm mush and empathetic tears rolled down her cheeks as she stared at the beautiful gift he was about to deliver to his parents.

"Are you crying?" Brian reached for her wrist before she could move away. "You are! But you never cry, Beth Crosby. You think it's unprofessional, and you've done it twice today."

His stunned expression was vastly overdone and belied by the teasing twinkle in his eyes. Fascinated by the mobility of features that had been slack for so long, Beth had to fight hard to regain her composure. It came as a shock that he knew her so well. Then again, why shouldn't he? He might not have been able to talk or move, but he'd registered everything she'd said or done for the past six months.

With a small tug, she tried to reclaim her hand. Brian wouldn't let go. Beth could have easily overcome his resistance but she didn't feel there was anything to gain by demonstrating her still superior strength. Instead she admitted shakily, "I might be a professional, but I'm as prone to tears as the next person. Who wouldn't cry under circumstances like this? I'm witness to a miracle."

"It is, isn't it," Brian replied, laughing, refusing to succumb to his own need to cry. He knew that in the next few minutes he'd be drowning in a flood of tears, his own included, and he needed Beth to be his lifeline in the emotional storm. He gave her fingers a gentle squeeze. "I never thought I'd see the day when my thick-skinned P.T. would shed a tear for me. I wonder how I can best take advantage of this sentimental weakness I've discovered. Play on her sympathies to get my own way?"

"You would, too, wouldn't you?" Beth scolded, thankful to him for ensuring that his parents wouldn't walk in and find her bawling like a baby. "Forewarned is forearmed, cowboy. Now let go of my hand."

"Okay, but if your poor fingers ever get stiff on the job, give me a call. I know of some wonderful exercises for each joint, learned at the feet of a cruel but very wise master." Reluctantly he let the soft, feminine hand slide through his fingers.

"I don't recall your ever being at my feet, Brian," Beth commented, feeling on safer ground as she shoved her hands in the back pockets of her jeans. She continued facetiously, "If you ever are at my feet, I'll expect you to kiss them in eternal gratitude."

"Your feet and anything else you'll let me kiss," Brian offered sweetly, but before he could savor her astounded reaction to the remark, his parents walked into the room. "Hi, Mom. Hi, Dad," he greeted them, as if it had been five minutes instead of five years since he'd last talked to them.

Glenda and Hadley froze midstride. Their faces drained instantly of all color. Mouths agape, eyes wide, they stared across the room as if seeing a ghost. Glenda was the first to recover.

"Oh, dear God! Brian!" Glenda flew across the room, tears glistening in her eyes. "Brian . . ."

Brian laughed and opened his arms. His mother responded in the same way Beth had, by throwing herself against Brian's chest, laughing and crying all over him. Hadley remained in the entryway watching the scene, seemingly incapable of moving.

Beth walked over to him and took his arm. "It's true, Mr. Towers. Brian has come out of it. In a few more months we'll hardly be able to tell how he's spent the past five years."

Hadley didn't budge, resisting the gentle pull on his arm. Beth was proud of herself for not dissolving back into tears at the sight of Brian's reunion with his mother, but with one look at his father's face she felt them threatening again. The man's features seemed to crumple before her eyes, emphasizing the deep creases and lines he'd acquired since Brian's accident. Suddenly he looked a hundred years old.

"Dad?" Brian called, lifting one hand from his mother's back to wave his father toward him. "I'm okay, Dad. It's true. I'm really okay."

Hadley didn't answer the call in a way any one of them would have expected. Before Beth could prevent it, he dropped to his knees on the floor, and his broad shoulders shaking, he started to weep. Beth felt she was intruding on a very private moment, hearing the distraught words of prayer and thanksgiving Hadley uttered between racking sobs.

Aware of the tortured sounds her husband was making, Glenda lifted her head from Brian's chest. Her face was transformed by a joy so great it was difficult to look at her. She and Brian exchanged a quick glance of total understanding, then swiftly she got to her feet. Reaching Hadley, she knelt beside him, wrapped her arms around him and pressed his head to her breast. With tears of happiness streaming down her face, she consoled her husband with the unfailing strength that had bolstered both him and their son for so long.

As Beth backed quietly away, she heard Glenda whisper, "Our prayers have been answered, darling. At last all our prayers have been answered and everything's going to be fine."

"Come here, Beth," Brian suggested, his voice roughened by emotion. "Let's give them a few minutes."

Beth nodded, unable to speak. She closed the French doors to the family room, shutting out the scene she had no right to witness. Her dark hazel eyes were shadowed, but the gold glints were shining through the bright shimmer of her tears as she sat down in the chair across from Brian. Soon, very soon for each of them, laughter would replace all their tears.

"I knew they'd react like that, especially Dad. This has been harder on him than on anyone."

Beth was amazed that Brian could be so understanding after the way his father had treated him while he was locked in. At times Hadley had looked at Brian as if he hated him for his helplessness, for being unable to take part in the bright future Hadley had planned. Beth had understood that the man was grief-stricken, but had often thought him selfish. Hadley had behaved as if his unhappiness were greater than Brian's, his suffering more painful, and in the past few weeks she could count his visits to Brian on one hand.

Her feelings must have been written on her face, for Brian immediately sprang to his father's defense. "Beth, some people can't deal with pain, especially not when it's being endured by people they love. I know you think it was wrong of him not to spend a lot of time with me, but it killed him just to look at me. If a child of mine ever had to go through something like this, I can't guarantee I won't react the same way. Can you?"

Beth considered how she'd react if she were the mother of a child in trauma, a child who might never awaken again. She would hope that she would remain strong and behave as Glenda had. But could she guarantee such support?

To be honest, the answer was no, and she experienced a surge of compassion for Brian's father. Brian had been restored to him, but now he'd always feel guilt for not being there when his son needed him most. "Only you'd know the best way to deal with it, Brian. Unlike any of us, you've been there."

"My dad would have given anything if it had been him and not me," Brian inserted quietly, studying her with tender anxiety that melted her heart.

"I know." Beth nodded. Her smile of understanding touched off the tiny dimple in her left cheek and deepened the gold in her eyes. "You're one incredible man, Brian Towers."

Brian's answering smile wasn't nearly as bright as Beth's. Mentally he added to her statement, *Or you will be when you grow up.* Somehow he had to prove to her that he was a mature adult, because he loved her not as an uninitiated youth but as a man.

He might not be equal to her in sophistication, social skills or sexual experience, but the past five years had taught him many things she had yet to learn. The most important lesson being that all feelings—love, anger, hatred, joy—were meant to be shared. He had done without sharing for too long; never would he allow himself to be so destitute again. Soon Beth was going to know exactly how he felt about her, whether she was prepared for the declaration or not.

In the meantime, he had a celebration to start. He shouted toward the closed French doors, "Hey, you two! What's a guy gotta do to get a decent meal around here?"

3

"I'M HAVIN' a Big Mac attack," Brian spouted gleefully. "I want some food I can sink my teeth into. I want some good old, all-American food that tastes like something. No more wallpaper paste for me! I want a beer, French fries, pizza, steak, chocolate brownies, Twinkies, onion rings, fried chicken, a hot fudge sundae, Coke, Seven-Up, a baked potato with a mountain of sour cream and bacon crumbles—"

"Stop! Stop," Beth begged laughingly. She puffed out her cheeks in a mock attack of nausea. "You're making me sick."

The French doors had swung open at Brian's first calls. Despite their tear-stained cheeks, Glenda and Hadley smiled broadly as their son chanted, "I want food. Bring me food."

Glenda began to laugh. "He's really all right."

Hadley's laughter joined his wife's. "Our boy's back. That's for sure."

Brian began listing the foods he craved, but once again Beth stopped him. "Okay. Okay. What do you really want for your first meal?"

"A triple order of everything. I've had five years of famine and I'm going to make up for it." He rubbed his palms together in anticipation and licked his lips. "I'll settle for a Coors beer and some potato chips until you can get the rest of the stuff. Then just keep it coming."

Before taking any steps to fulfill her son's request, Glenda turned to Beth. "What do you think?"

"I spoke to Dr. Samuels and he said Brian can have anything he wants, within reason," Beth assured her. "His stomach isn't used to much bulk or heavy seasonings. A broiled chicken breast and a baked potato wouldn't be too much of a shock to his system. We'll have to see about dessert."

"Hey!" Brian interjected. "It's my stomach and I'll decide what goes in it. Now order a pizza and send somebody out to the closest McDonald's."

Beth resisted his request. "Brian, you really can't assault your gastrointestinal system with junk food. Your body will revolt and you'll—"

"My body will do what I tell it to," he announced stubbornly. "Nobody, including you, is going to decide what I eat ever again! Now would you please get Jake or somebody in here to take my order. Mom, how 'bout that chicken? Dad, you wanta have a beer with me?"

Hadley stepped past the two women and toward the bar in the far corner of the room. "It'll be like old times, son," he said with a shaky grin as he extracted two golden cans from the refrigerator and a bag of potato chips from a cupboard beneath the oak bar. "But, Brian, you really shouldn't overindulge today. Beth is right. It's been five years since you've had any of this stuff. Let's forgo the pizza for the time being. You've got to be patient and—"

"Patient? Damn it, I've had five years of being a patient and I'm not wasting any more of my life!"

Brian grasped the arms of his chair and pulled himself to his feet. "Hell, I'll order the pizza myself." He lurched across the room toward the telephone on the desk. As soon as he reached the nearest wall, he slumped against the gleaming wood and waited for his legs to stop shaking; they didn't and he began slithering to the floor.

Beth and his parents rushed to his aid.

"Leave me alone," Brian snarled, and waved them away. "I don't need or want anybody's help."

He tried to push himself off the floor, but met with little success. Sweat beaded on his forehead and his breath came in gasps as he rolled himself to an all-fours position and started crawling toward the desk.

The joy of Brian's recovery disappeared in the face of his anger and frustration. Glenda's eyes filled with tears and she covered her quivering lips with her hand when Brian collapsed on his stomach, then continued dragging himself with his forearms. His progress was torturously slow, but inch by painful inch he moved toward his goal. His face tight, Hadley watched Brian's desperate efforts. Not knowing what to do, he looked to Beth for guidance.

Initially as immobilized by Brian's behavior as the Towers's, Beth forced herself into action. She quietly directed Hadley to find Jake and bring him to the room.

Placing an arm around Glenda's shoulders, she guided her toward the door and whispered a gentle suggestion that she go see about the chicken. The Towerses meekly left and Beth went to Brian. Dropping to her knees beside him, she placed a firm hand on one of his shoulders.

"Brian," Beth said, biting her lip when she felt him shudder beneath her touch. "Stop this . . . now."

Brian dropped his chest and head to the floor, turning his face away from her. He lay there panting for several moments before saying, "I'm acting like a spoiled kid, aren't I?"

Beth replied matter-of-factly, "It's understandable. You'd reached the end of your tether."

Instinctively she began to massage his back, her palm moving in soothing circles. "It's been a long five years, longer for you than for any of us. We can't possibly know all you've been feeling during this time. I can only imagine how frustrating it's been not having any means of venting your anger, desperation and utter hopelessness."

"It was like being in prison." Brian spoke to the wall. "No . . . worse. I felt like the 'man in the iron mask.' But at least he could move his body, make some noise."

"Oh, Brian," she whispered, tears of empathy welling up in her eyes.

She became aware of a presence beside her. Somehow, despite his size, Jake had glided without a sound into the room. She raised her hand, her fingers spread wide in a signal she hoped Jake would understand meant she wanted a little time. Beth hoped to be able to coax Brian into accepting some help. His self-esteem had been given a severe blow and he didn't need to be wounded any further.

Surprising Beth with his intuitive understanding, Jake left the room as silently as he'd arrived.

"Brian?" she coaxed. "Please look at me."

From force of habit, Brian blinked once. *No.*

"Brian . . ." Beth leaned back on her heels, sensing what he was doing. "Don't shut me out, mister. You don't have that luxury anymore."

Brian turned his head sharply, his expression thunderous. "Luxury? Lying in a bed for five years and being able to do nothing but blink my damned eyes was no luxury. Sometimes I was screaming and nobody knew it. I wanted to throw things, punch somebody, laugh, and all I could do was—" He blinked his eyes frantically. "Blink. Blink. Blink."

"But you could pull in whenever you wanted to. You could ignore people and nobody ever accused you of being rude," Beth fired back. "Okay, so you were stuck in a cocoon. A nice, safe cocoon where nobody demanded anything of you. You're not in there anymore. You're out, and I'm not going to let you climb back in."

Brian glared at Beth and read the determination in her eyes, but didn't relent. He had a right to be angry. "You're damned right I'm not climbing back into hell."

"Good!" Beth smiled. "You're going to work more than your eyelid muscles from now on, cowboy. You're going to start off by telling me exactly what kind of pizza you want."

Brian stared at her, his mouth agape, his temper abruptly diffused. "Come here," he ordered with a hoarse growl.

"I am here."

"Not close enough, and I'm too tired to grab you and pull you down here for a kiss."

It was Beth's turn to stare, mouth agape. "Uh . . . Brian . . ."

"Please, Beth. Just a little kiss. I need it." He hated himself for pleading for something as simple as a kiss, especially when he'd just lost every shred of his pride. He rolled to his back. "I'm harmless," he admitted with a wry grin. "I don't have any energy left. I need another jolt to my system to wake it up."

"I don't have magic kisses, Brian," she protested. "I shouldn't have kissed you earlier today. That was highly—"

"Unprofessional?" he finished for her, and Beth wanted to crawl beneath the carpet. Guiltily she glanced over her shoulder to make sure they were still alone. They were, to her great relief.

"Yes, it was unprofessional," Beth confirmed. "And I'm not going to compound the error by repeating it."

"Stop feeling guilty," he ordered quietly, looking up into her face and delving beyond the barriers she was trying to put up. "I'm sure not sorry, and I'm begging you to do it again." He lifted an unsteady hand and trailed his fingertips along her jaw. "Please, just a small gesture of human caring." His voice was low, hoarse, and his words were halting.

Beth was finding it very difficult to resist the entreaty in his tone. And in his eyes. In the months she'd worked with him, his eyes had sometimes smote her, and sometimes they'd called out to her. They were calling to her now, reaching beyond the therapist for the woman.

Against her better judgment, Beth leaned over and brushed her lips across Brian's. Her closed mouth was pressed to his for only a second, the kiss no more passionate than one that would be bestowed on a child. It was a touch, a reassurance, and Brian's lips remained passive beneath hers. Yet the contact was far from harmless.

Beth had spent the past six months running her hands over Brian's body. She was almost as familiar with it as she was with her own. Yet when he'd been locked in, he had lain immobile and his muscles had been flacid. Now his body was full of energy, every line tense, geared for motion. He was no longer a helpless patient but a man.

Though his lips hadn't moved beneath hers, they'd been firm and vibrant; the pent-up energy and vitality of the man transmitted itself all the way to her toes. When she sat back on her heels, Beth felt as if she'd experienced a far greater intimacy than a brief kiss.

Brian kept his eyes closed, savoring the feathery imprint of the too short caress. "Thanks. I needed that." He let out a long sigh, a sign of both physical and emotional exhaustion. "You can go ahead and let Jake back in now. No more tantrums tonight." He opened one eye and grinned mischievously. "Unless you put green peppers and anchovies on that pizza you're going to order."

Still shaken by the kiss, Beth took a moment to assimilate the abrupt change of subject. "You still want that pizza?"

"Yep. And all the rest of it."

"You're going to be sorry," she warned.

"Not as sorry as you'll be if you don't get that pizza ordered."

Within an hour, Brian was sitting at the dining room table, which was laden with an assortment of paper sacks, cartons and foil-wrapped "delicacies." Tempering his order for triple everything, he had agreed to settle for a single of everything he'd requested. A blissful smile spread across his face as he breathed in the mingled aromas of the carryout foods spread before him. "The smell of all this stuff is a treat in itself," he announced as he reached for a wedge of pizza.

He took his first bite of the spicy food. His eyes twinkled with joy and satisfaction as he savored the strong flavors. "Wake up taste buds. Your vacation is over. You're about to have a feast fit for a gourmet."

"More like a binge for a glutton," Hadley commented.

Beth, Glenda and Hadley sat on the other sides of the table, anxiety and disapproval evident on their faces. Brian had already polished off the chicken and baked potato Glenda had prepared for him and shared a beer with his father while he'd waited for the arrival of what he'd deemed the "real food."

"Brian, maybe you ought to take just one bite of each thing," Beth ventured. "There's an awful lot of food here."

Brian wiped the tomato sauce from the corners of his mouth, then stared at the white paper napkin in his hand. "You're right," he said absently, still staring at the napkin.

He looked at his mother, back to the napkin, and chuckled. "You probably won't believe this, Mom, but I'm honestly glad to be able to use a napkin again."

Glenda's light laughter joined her son's. "Oh, Brian. You used to think napkins were the greatest waste of time when the back of your hand or your sleeve would do as well."

"You used to say that using a napkin properly was not only polite but the sign of an independent adult," he reminded her with obvious pleasure.

Glenda shrugged, her smile lighting up her face. "I was desperate."

"You were right." Brian looked back at the napkin again, studying it and moving his fingers against its texture. "Wiping your own mouth is a very independent thing. God, I really am going to be taking care of myself from now on," he said, more to himself then to anyone else.

Hadley cleared his throat. "Speaking of good manners, son. Are you going to keep all this to yourself, or are you willing to share some of the bounty? All this excitement has whet my appetite."

Brian halted the progress of a French fry toward his mouth. "Haven't you folks eaten?" He watched three heads shake. Pushing the flat pizza carton toward the center of the table, he invited, "Dig in." He patted his stomach sheepishly, then winked at Beth. "I don't think I'm ready to take on all of this."

Beth grinned, the dimple in her left cheek twinkling, but she refrained from saying "I told you so" aloud. However, she and Brian had never needed words to communicate. From the slight shrug of his shoulders she knew he'd gotten her message.

From that point on, Brian's celebratory meal changed from a one-man exhibition to a shared experience. Though he was determined to have a portion of everything, Beth noticed that as time went on his bites became smaller and smaller. Beneath the table, she crossed her fingers that his wisdom hadn't come too late. By the end of the meal, she wanted to suggest he top everything off with a glass of Alka Seltzer. She remembered his earlier declaration that from now on he'd decide what went into his stomach, though, and remained silent.

Leaning back in his chair, a look of satisfaction on his face, Brian asked, "What day is it?"

"Monday," Hadley supplied.

"Monday night baseball," Brian announced with a grin. He pushed himself away from the table and started to get up. His legs had other ideas, however, and didn't support him. Plopping back into his chair, he tightened his lips for a fraction of a second and then smiled. "Ah . . . somebody want to volunteer to help me back to the family room?"

"I'll call Jake," Glenda immediately suggested.

"No." Hadley's negative stopped his wife. He stood up from the table and walked around to stand beside his son. He dropped his hand to Brian's shoulder. "I'll do it. You can lean on me, son."

"I know, Dad," Brian said as he looked up to his father. "I've always known that." He reached up and placed his hand over Hadley's.

Hadley helped Brian out of the chair. With Brian's arm draped over his shoulder and his own wrapped firmly around his son's waist, he started off toward the family room with Brian. "It'll be like old times, Brian," he said as they went through the doorway. "The Reds aren't playing tonight, but there's still a baseball game. Do you mind?"

"I don't care who's playing as long as I can sit in a regular room in a regular chair and work the channel selector myself."

Glenda waited until she was sure neither of them could hear her. Tears were once again streaming down her cheeks and her fragile shoulders shook. "Oh, Beth, how can we ever thank you? You've brought him back."

"No, Glenda," Beth said, uncomfortable with the older woman's estimation of her abilities. "Brian did this himself. He wanted to come back. I only—"

"Only?" Glenda interrupted as she mopped her face with her napkin. "You're an extraordinary young woman, Beth Crosby. You're the best friend this family has been privileged to have. You kept our hopes up. Don't ever try to belittle the part you played in bringing Brian back to us. I'm as happy as I was the day he was born."

Beth nodded. "In some ways he has been reborn. He's far from helpless, but he's still going to have to relearn a lot of things."

"What exactly did Dr. Samuels say?" Glenda queried. "I'm surprised he didn't get right out here."

"He'll be out tomorrow morning right after he makes his hospital rounds," Beth explained. "He felt that psychologically it would be better for Brian if he were able to enjoy this evening without a doctor hovering over him. According to Dr. Samuels, Brian's heart is strong and he's in very good health. He may tire far more quickly than he's going to like, though, and his muscles are going to be screaming at him tomorrow."

"You think he'll last through the game?" Glenda asked, nodding in the direction of the family room. She smiled when she heard a duet of male voices shout, "All right! Home run!"

"Let's go join them and find out," Beth suggested.

Brian's energy steadily waned as the game progressed. By the third inning, he'd pulled the lever on the recliner chair and brought up the footrest. By the bottom of the fourth inning, the back of the chair had been pushed down a notch or two. By the top of the sixth, Brian was fast asleep, and Hadley sent for Jake.

As the large, taciturn man lifted him from the chair, Brian came awake. "Don't carry me," he mumbled sleepily. "You can help me, but don't ever carry me again."

Jake nodded and let Brian's feet drop to the floor. Supporting most of Brian's weight, Jake helped him from the room. Brian didn't offer any more words of complaint until he and Jake passed the staircase leading to the second floor. "Wait a minute. I'm not sleeping in that damned hospital bed. I want my own bed," he announced firmly, and stopped moving his feet. Though Jake could have easily forced him to continue toward the first-floor accommodations, he obligingly gave in.

"But Brian," Glenda inserted gently. As had both Hadley and Beth, she'd come into the hall as soon as they'd heard Brian's demand. "Your room hasn't been used in five years. It needs fresh linens and—"

"Then get some," Brian said simply. He pushed away from Jake and settled himself on the steps. Looking up at his mother, he smiled the lopsided smile that came so naturally to him. "Sorry, Mom. Would you please have some sheets put on my bed? I'd like to wake up in that room and know that today and this evening wasn't just a dream."

"Brian," Beth began as she came forward. "There's no reason why you can't sleep in your own bed, except that it's on the second floor. Are you willing to let Jake carry you up those stairs and back down tomorrow morning?"

Brian turned his irresistible smile full force on Beth. "What'll you do if I say no?"

"Cut off your pizza supply," she threatened with mock seriousness.

"I was afraid of that." Crossing his arms over his chest, he settled his shoulders against the wall. "Okay, okay. Jake can carry me up there tonight."

"And tomorrow morning? Will you promise to stay put until he comes for you?" Beth didn't trust his acquiescence; he had a stubborn streak a mile long. She'd guessed it from the first, and since he'd "come out," her suspicion had been confirmed. She also suspected he could be very wily.

Resting his head against the wall, Brian closed his eyes. Beth was sure he was resorting to his old tricks. "Brian . . . ?"

"Not shutting down. Promise. I'm just sleepy and I want to spend the night in my own bed."

Brian's face reflected his fatigue. All the healthy color that had risen in his cheeks with the excitement of today's events had faded away. Beth wasn't surprised that he was having trouble holding his head up and keeping his eyes open. Though she still didn't trust that he wouldn't try to maneuver the stairs by himself tomorrow morning, she didn't press the issue. "Okay, you can sleep in your own bed."

"I'll put the sheets on, darling," Glenda quickly volunteered. "You wait right there. It won't take long." She bent and kissed her son's forehead before starting up the stairs.

"Not going anyplace," Brian mumbled, moving his head from side to side, searching for the most comfortable position.

Beth followed Glenda up the stairs. Between the two of them, readying Brian's room for occupancy didn't take long. As with all the rooms in the Towers mansion, Brian's was always kept in perfect order.

As she slipped a pillow into a fresh case, Beth remembered the first time she'd seen the room. Glenda had included it as part of the tour of the house on Beth's first day on the job.

Wallpaper in a navy, cream and taupe plaid covered the bottom third of the walls. A chair rail set off the upper portion of ivory, textured plaster. Thick, tweed carpet covered the floor. The furniture was all heavy wood. Framed certificates, team pictures, a few individual shots of Brian in full football gear, and shelves of trophies were arranged on all the walls. A large poster of a rock group popular several years ago was pinned to a bulletin board.

It was a typical room of a high school athlete, which was exactly what Brian had been when he'd last occupied it. During two brief years after high school, Brian had lived on campus and been more a visitor to this room than its official resident.

Glenda finished smoothing the sheets and then she, too, turned her attention to her surroundings. "It's not exactly the kind of room a twenty-five-year-old man should occupy is it? Funny, I never considered changing it before."

She ran her fingertips lightly over a picture of Brian in his scarlet-and-gray uniform. Brian had a football tucked protectively under one arm, his body poised as if to run. His jaw was set as if daring anyone to try to snatch the ball from him.

"He was strong, so full of life. I haven't been able to really look at this picture for a very long time," Glenda said slowly. She took a deep breath and straightened her shoulders. "The past is best left in the past. It's time to look to the future."

"It'll have to wait till tomorrow," Hadley said from the doorway. "We've got a very tired b—man to put to bed."

"That bed looks wonderful," Brian breathed as Jake helped him toward it. "Any pj's left in the dresser?"

Glenda whisked a pair of cotton pajamas from the second drawer as if she'd just put them there the day before. She gave them a shake and placed them next to Brian on the bed.

After wishing Brian a good night, everyone but Jake headed for the door. Before leaving, Beth offered, "I'm right next door if you need anything during the night. Otherwise you can use the intercom and call Jake."

Brian's eyes told her that no matter what need might arise in the hours before morning, he'd handle it himself. She waggled a knowing finger at him. "I mean it, Brian."

"Uh-huh," he agreed, but both were aware of the odds of his calling upon her or anybody else.

Hours later, Beth was awakened by the sound of Brian's retching coming from the bathroom between their two rooms. She got out of bed, intending to rush through the connecting door, but something stopped her, some inner sense that told her Brian wouldn't welcome her help. Unless he was in desperate need, it would be wiser if she stayed in her own room. Brian wanted his independence and needed his privacy. The most she should do was alert Jake.

She waited for several more minutes, her anxiety growing. There was silence from the neighboring bedroom. Was Brian all right? Had he passed out in the bathroom? Fallen down and hit his head on the tub or sink?

Her hand was on the doorknob of the bathroom, but before she could turn it, she heard Jake's heavy tred on the stairs. A few moments later, she again heard Brian through the wall, suffering for his excesses at the dinner table. All that was in her urged her to go to him, but she forced herself to return to bed. Jake was with him. Jake would take care of him.

Brian may have demonstrated some imprudence with his first meal, but by calling Jake, he'd shown commendable judgment. She could drop her vigilance and relax, secure in the knowledge that her presence wasn't necessary. Even so, one ear remained tuned to the room next to hers for the rest of the night.

4

A MUFFLED SOUND from the hallway awakened Beth from a light sleep. Glancing at her bedside table, she saw that it was barely six o'clock. It was rare for any member of the Towers household to be up and about before seven, so she had a very good idea who might be creeping around in the early morning hours. If she was right, that person was in for a stern lecture from his physical therapist. Considering the night Brian had put in, she was amazed he had enough energy left to get up at all this morning.

Hopping out of bed, Beth paused only long enough to don a thin robe over her pink shortie nightgown before opening the door and peeking outside. Brian was poised at the top of the stairs. If she didn't stop him, he was apt to take a header and very probably reinjure himself.

She thought of the promise he'd neatly avoided making the night before, and shook her head. It was obvious that he had no intention of staying put ever again. She could sympathize, but only up to a point.

Beth slipped silently out of the room, her bare feet making no noise on the Oriental runner that stretched down the middle of the hall.

"Where do you think you're going?" she asked quietly, not wanting to startle him as she came up behind him.

Brian groaned at the sound of her voice. He glanced over his shoulder at her, then back down at the quivering muscles in his arms. He had taken a death grip on the carved walnut newel at the top of the stairs. His legs were shaking so badly that if he let go of the post, he knew he'd fall down. Even as it was, he didn't know how long he could maintain his semiupright position.

His expression said it all. He was angry with her for catching him in the act of doing something stupid, but more angry with himself for not being able to get away with it. "I'm on my way out to the pool," he stated in a tone that dared her to contradict him.

"Is that right?" Beth replied, biting the inside of her lower lip to prevent the sharp rejoinder that was poised on the tip of her tongue. Crossing her arms over her chest, she cocked her head and studied his seemingly romantic attachment to the thick post. "And how were you proposing to do that?"

No response.

Beth took a step forward and leaned back against the opposite post as if to get a better view of the dilemma posed to him by the long flight of stairs. She considered the distance to the first floor, then studied his quaking lower limbs. "I suppose you could throw one leg over the railing and slide down the banister."

That helpful suggestion inspired another black scowl. Beth hid her reaction to the sight of it. She had discovered yesterday and today that watching a face that had been immobile for months and years exhibit any kind of emotion, even anger, was utterly fascinating. She couldn't let Brian know that, however. She had enough trouble on her hands without his being aware that she found every nuance of his expression a visual treat.

"Mmmm," she murmured thoughtfully, a golden sparkle dancing in her eyes. "No, I can see that the banister idea wouldn't work. You don't have enough strength yet to maintain your balance all the way down. I guess you'll just have to do it the way babies do. Roll over on your tummy and slide down feet first."

"Beth!" Brian warned, furious that she should find him in such a vulnerable position and take such joy in rubbing it in.

Undeterred by his menacing tone, Beth continued, "I taught my eight-month-old neice to go down the stairs that way. I suppose I could teach you. At least, I think you might be able to match her intelligence."

"Very funny," he grunted as his legs gave way and he slithered down into a half sitting, half kneeling position. Shoulders propped against the post, he cast a baleful eye up at her. "What did you do? Sit up all night with your ear tuned to the door? Is that why I've been blessed with your uninvited and unwelcome presence?"

Lips twitching, Beth sat down facing him on the top step. "My, my, we certainly are surly this morning, aren't we?"

Irritation flared hotter in his eyes. "You're going to keep on patronizing me until I admit I should have stayed in bed until Jake came up to get me, aren't you?"

"Confucius say, where logic fails, condescension shall prosper."

Brian sighed. "You made that up."

Lifting her shoulders in a noncommittal shrug, Beth credited the ancient Chinese philosopher with another saying. "A wise man knows that to go beyond is as wrong as to fall short. A child does both, and often falls down stairs or upchucks his dinner."

Brian leaned his head back on the post to hide his unwilling smile. All those months when he couldn't move, Beth had been adept at turning his anger to stoic acceptance. At times, he'd have burst out laughing at something she'd said if only his unresponsive body would have allowed it. Now that he had his functions back, she was going to find out exactly how much he appreciated her dry sense of humor. Knowing her, she'd take full advantage of that knowledge.

Meanwhile, he intended to qualify his own position. "Beth?"

"What?"

"In the past six months, how many arguments have you allowed me to win?"

"I wasn't aware we had any arguments," Beth replied, then amended. "At least not any serious ones."

"It didn't matter to me whether they were serious," Brian continued in the same vein and in the same grim tone. "I always got the short end of the stick. From now on, I won't let you or anyone else ignore my opinions. That was one of the most emasculating things I had to endure through this whole thing. My opinion didn't count worth a damn.

"Someone else decided what I should wear, when I should eat and drink, when I should study or exercise, even when I should relieve myself. If I hadn't come out of this when I did, you would have started those shock treatments no matter how I felt about it."

Beth understood how hard it must have been for him, but still defended herself and his family. "You know all we wanted to do was help you, Brian, since you couldn't help yourself." She paused for a few seconds, then admitted, "I probably would have tried electro-therapy even without your permission. Electrical stimulation has achieved some very good results in cases like yours."

Brian looked directly into her eyes, speaking to her without words even though he could now say whatever he chose. Beth could tell that he wasn't angry with her, nor was he holding a grudge for anything she might have done against his will in the course of his treatment. On the other hand, the set of his jaw and the resolute light in his blue eyes told her she no longer enjoyed a position of unquestioned authority. If she wanted his future cooperation, there would have to be compromises.

"Why was it so important that you make it out to the pool this morning under your own power?"

Brian smiled at the question, aware that her intuition was as strong as ever. A cruel stroke of fate had taken virtually everything away from him, but ultimately had provided him with a woman whose uncanny ability to read his mind had saved him from utter despair. He owed her so much, and couldn't start paying her back until he'd regained his strength.

Patience had never been his strong suit and he refused to tolerate any more pity—especially from her. "I'm taking control of my own life, Beth. I'm a man, and from now on I intend to be treated like one," he stated firmly, even as his lips curved in a self-mocking smile. "I thought I'd prove that this morning. Unfortunately, the mind might be willing, but the body is still weak."

"When the chips are down, even a man who's in complete control of his life will accept a little help from his friends," Beth reminded him.

Beth knew why he was so reluctant to accept that estimation of his position. He'd had enough help to last him a lifetime. Even so, until his strength and stamina were fully restored, he must accept more. She pointed down the stairs and reminded, "Pride goeth before a fall."

Brian groaned. "My folks went out to find a physical therapist and brought back a half-baked philosopher."

Beth wrinkled her nose at him. "I can't help it if bountiful wisdom falls from my lips like honey."

"And tastes like it."

"Come again?" Beth asked, and immediately regretted the question. Brian was staring at her mouth, his gaze intensely disturbing.

"Your lips taste like the sweetest honey," he returned, matching the warmth of his tone to the heat in his eyes as they traveled down her slender body. "I wonder if your skin does, too."

He scooted across the floor, one leg stretched out on the top three stairs, the other touching hers. He bent his head toward the side of her neck and inhaled. "Mmmm, today it's lemons. Yesterday was roses and the day before that violets. I am here to attest that any one of those delicious scents can drive a guy over the edge."

He lifted his head before he gave in to the urge to nuzzle his face between her soft, full breasts, where he knew the scent of her perfume would be strongest. He had gained proof of that whenever she'd leaned over to adjust a pillow or massage his neck. Recalling those times, he also remembered how often he'd fantasized about her standing naked before a mirror, applying sweet smelling perfume to her breasts and the shadowed satiny flesh between them.

He'd pictured her nipples, pink and pouting, waiting for possession by a man's mouth—his mouth. His lips would caress her, his tongue encircle the delicate point, drawing her sweetness into himself. She would moan with pleasure, then cry out in need as he tantalized first one end and then the other with his teeth and tongue.

"Brian!"

He jumped at the alarmed tone of Beth's voice, abruptly aware that his eyes were focused greedily on those parts of her anatomy that had caused him so many hours of mental torture. "Don't look so shocked," he advised. "I was only looking."

Beth was shocked, speechless with shock. Both hands clutched the material of her robe and she pulled the two edges tightly over her breasts. She had to breath but didn't dare, fearing he would see how affected she'd been by his caressing gaze.

She had prided herself on being able to read what was in his eyes. Why had she never been aware of the kind of passion she had witnessed in them the past few seconds? It was obvious he'd had such erotic thoughts before.

Just looking? His gaze was hot, intimate, as if he were familiar with every inch of her body. It was the gaze of a longtime lover and made her feel as if he'd actually reached out and touched her, kissed her naked breasts. Had he done so in his mind? Frequently?

Not yet ready to face that possibility, Beth looked down, and immediately wished she hadn't. By tightening her robe, she'd merely enhanced the evidence of her arousal. She curved her spine, allowing more space between her taut nipples and the soft fabric of her robe. She drew in a deep breath. "Yes . . . well, if you're as anxious to make rapid progress as you say you are, you'll have to find something more constructive to do with your time."

Getting to her feet, she started down the stairs. "I'll go get Jake. He can help you out to the pool. Then this afternoon we can start you on a regimen of exercises that will have you back to normal in no time."

"Beth."

She turned around at the base of the stairs and looked up to where he was sitting, legs drawn up, chin in palms, watching her. "Yes."

He flicked an audacious glance at her bosom, then back to her flushed cheeks. "I'm very satisfied with the progress I've already made today."

Deliberately misinterpreting his statement, she shook a finger at him. "Too bad. It's back to therapy for you, cowboy, and the sooner the better."

His answering chuckle was husky and low, extremely suggestive and very, very male.

Practically running on her way to find Jake, Beth prayed that the water in the pool would be cold—ice-cold.

WHEN BETH ARRIVED in the therapy room later that morning, Brian and Jake were out of the pool, had had breakfast and were hard at work. She was grateful to see that Brian had exchanged his skimpy trunks for a baggy gray sweatsuit. Now they were both dressed appropriately for the upcoming work session and they could direct their energies in the proper direction.

Immediately after talking with Dr. Samuels the previous day, Beth had placed a rush order for a set of parallel bars, a treadmill, an incline bench, an exercycle and a leg lift and weights. Even so, she was amazed that the equipment had already arrived and was ready for use. After he was finished with Brian, Jake must have stayed up the rest of the night putting it all together.

It seemed strange to watch Brian walking in place on the treadmill instead of lying on the bed. Working with him in his mobile condition was going to require some readjustment in her thinking, as well as in the routine of exercises she'd been using up until now. She realized that due to his age, condition and overall good health, his physical recovery would be rapid. She could only hope that emotionally he would do as well.

If the unnerving episode on the stairs was any example of his underlying attitude toward her, she was going to be in for some difficult times. Even though he'd been unable to respond over the past month, he'd been mentally recording every incident that had taken place between them. Considering how close they'd become, she shouldn't have been surprised when he'd revealed his attraction to her. Misplaced affection was the normal result of lengthy, intimate interaction between a patient and therapist. Still, knowing that fact and dealing with it were two entirely different matters.

Brian turned off the treadmill and spied Beth hovering in the doorway. He swallowed a chuckle as he made note of her outfit. Until today, she'd shown up every morning in a pair of tight jeans and a T-shirt. This morning, a crisp blue linen smock covered her usual outfit. Evidently she hoped the introduction of a uniform would help keep their relationship on a professional level. That hope would be short-lived.

"Can you go get me some orange juice, Jake?" Brian requested as he lowered himself on the incline bench, ostensibly to retie the laces of his running shoes.

"Sure." Jake said, and left the room.

"Are you coming in or not?" Brian looked up, grinning when Beth took a few steps into the room. She surveyed the new equipment, commented on Jake's diligent handiwork, but she didn't approach Brian. He could almost hear her brain working, striving to come up with an appropriate speech that would warn him to keep his distance. He decided to help her out.

Eyeing her smock, he remarked casually, "I've always been a sucker for a girl in uniform."

Beth marched toward him, arms crossed over her chest. Before she could launch into her intended speech, he made another comment that sidetracked her. "You can wear a sack, cross both your arms and your legs, and I'll still know what you've got. I've had the same six months you've had to take inventory."

He could see by the high color in her cheeks that his use of her terms threw her, and that pleased him. If he kept her off-balance, he just might be able to slip in under her guard before she realized what was happening. No matter what she wanted him to think, he knew that she was just as attracted to him as he was to her.

As far as he was concerned, the only problem that presented was one of her own making. Regardless of whatever professional ethic she thought she was breaking, she was perfect for him and he was perfect for her. All he had to do was prove it.

Head cocked, he watched her digest the information he'd just given her, then gave her more to swallow. "I regret I was the only one to benefit from a hands-on inspection, but I expect that to change. Next time there's an inventory, these hands will be taking it." He flexed his fingers as if in anticipation.

Rather than stand before him like a sputtering idiot, so flustered she couldn't move, Beth sat down right next to him on the bench. She had spent the past hour preparing herself for just such a scene. With a completely natural gesture, she reached for his hand, squeezing it gently as she began talking. Reminding him of an old-fashioned schoolmarm, she told him exactly what he could expect from her in future. With every word she spoke, the more irritated he became.

"I'm your physical therapist, Brian," she informed him. "No more and no less. It's natural that you'd feel there was something more between us, given that I'm the only woman you've had any personal dealings with for so long, but what you're feeling for me isn't real. In a few more weeks, you'll go out and meet other women and be grateful I recognized the situation for what it was. You don't want me, Brian. You may think you do right now, but you won't once you've put your life back together again."

Brian snatched his hand away as soon as the last word left her lips. He stood up from the bench and rounded on her. "That's a lot of bull and you know it.

I don't know who you think you're fooling, Beth, but it isn't me."

Before she knew what he'd intended, he'd grabbed her by the shoulders and hauled her up in front of him. Beth was astonished by his strength and stunned by the blazing passion in his blue eyes. "I know what I want and I know what you want, both now and later, when my life's back together again. Please give me credit for a little intelligence."

Beth stared up into his face, too stunned by the look in his eyes to struggle. His mouth descended on hers with unerring precision, muffling the protest she'd been about to utter. Lips parted, eyes open, Beth brought up her hands to push him away, but her protests turned to helpless response.

Brian might have missed out on five years of social development, but he kissed like a man with a vast amount of experience. Expecting the wet, brutal assault of a sex-starved pseudoadolescent, Beth was caught off guard by Brian's refined attention to detail. His tongue tangled with hers in a wild, exquisite exploration, while his lips tasted her as if savoring a rare delicacy. His mouth was warm and hard, his lips tender, his technique flawless.

The more Brian gave the more Beth wanted, and she moaned with the knowledge that this flaming, rampaging, ever multiplying need couldn't be satisfied. She closed her eyes, shutting out the sight of finely drawn eyebrows, dark lashes tipped with gold, and the sweep of golden hair falling over a tanned forehead. She willed her spine to go stiff, applying pressure to his chest with her tightly clenched fists.

Brian let go of her by torturous degrees, conscious of her resistance, but equally aware of the sweet, feminine desire that lay so close beneath the surface of her rigid form. He had tasted it, felt it mounting in her, fighting for release. He looked down into her eyes and saw the last glimmers of gold before they were lost in pools of dark toffee. This time she had managed to bring her passion to heel.

He tried not to smile, knowing she would have to react angrily. She had great respect for the strict code of professional ethics, which would keep her from acknowledging what both of them knew had just happened. But her eyes gave her away. A new bond had been forged between them, and a powerful magnetic current that had nothing to do with the pull of friendship was growing stronger every day. He would make sure that it grew stronger still. "I could go on kissing you forever."

"You can't, Brian. We can't." Beth admitted her momentary lapse with admirable honesty, though her voice faltered and broke. When she saw his eyes darken, she hurried on, "We both have to remember what I said before you . . . Ours is a working relationship," she persisted. "It can't be anything else." But her body didn't move and his hands didn't drop away from her shoulders. They went on gazing into each other's eyes, passing messages neither one of them was willing to form into words. Finally Beth took a deep breath and repeated, "A *working* relationship."

Brian was about to tell her what areas he'd like to work on, when a booming male voice cut in from the doorway. "A little unsteady, are you Brian? You'll have to expect that for the next few weeks."

"Dr. Samuels!" Beth broke away from Brian with a guilty start. Her sudden movement threw him off-balance, and she instinctively reached out for him again. Her hands closed on his arms as he grabbed for the parallel bars behind him.

"Damn rubbery legs!"

Beth didn't know if Brian's evasive action was deliberate, but she was grateful in any case. The last person she wanted to have find her in a compromising position with a patient was that patient's doctor. At least now Jeffery Samuels would have some doubt about what he had just seen. *Please, Lord. Make him have some doubt.*

"Let's get you over to the bed so the doctor can examine you," Beth suggested, wiping all expression from her face as Brian lowered his arms over her shoulders. "Maybe he'll be able to convince you that you can't take on everything all at once."

"I doubt it," Jeff Samuels put in pointedly as he lifted his medical bag onto the foot of the bed.

After that comment, Beth refrained from looking at the young doctor who, over the past two years, had become a close friend. They had met when she was working at Riverside Hospital. When she'd applied to

Glenda Towers, he had added his recommendation. Jeff had supported her, no matter how unorthodox some of her ideas for Brian's treatment were. From the first he'd respected both her and her theories.

At thirty-five, he was more open-minded than many of his colleagues and had never been one to behave as if a doctor's opinion were etched in granite. Beth disliked deceiving him almost as much as she abhorred the thought of telling him the truth.

"I may not have my sea legs quite yet, but it's a miraculous improvement just the same," Brian said. With Beth's assistance, he was walking slowly and carefully toward the bed. "Wouldn't you say so, Doc?"

"Oh, I would," Jeff replied dryly. Assessing gray eyes passed from Beth's flushed cheeks to Brian's tight jaw. "A dream come true, I expect."

Brian shot him a questioning look as he removed his arm from Beth's shoulders and positioned his body on the mattress. Unable to read anything besides clinical interest in the doctor's expression, he embraced the role of humble patient with the mastery of a quick-change artist. "Thanks, Beth. You know your stuff and I appreciate your expert advice. From now on, I promise to do whatever the doctor orders."

"Sounds good to me," Jeff agreed as he hung a stethoscope around his neck. Butter wouldn't have melted in his mouth as he ordered his unusually cooperative patient to disrobe. "This is going to be a very thorough examination, Brian. It's going to take some time."

"Oh, wonderful," Brian growled, realizing what was to come.

Jeff chuckled as he took off his suit coat and rolled up his sleeves. Without taking his eyes off his patient, who was beginning to look a little green about the gills, he requested, "If you wouldn't mind, Beth, I'd like something cool to drink once I've finished in here."

"Not at all." Beth hastened to the door, as anxious to leave as Brian was to see her go. "How about a tall glass of iced tea?"

"Fine." Jeff didn't look at her again, but she didn't need to see his face in order to know that Brian's act hadn't fooled him one bit. "I'll meet you on the patio. I'd like to talk to you privately once I've assured myself that this fella is as raring to go as he looks."

An hour later, Brian stood at the window of the convalarium, gazing out at the two people seated on the patio. Heads together, shoulders touching, they were sharing cold drinks and a chaise longue by the pool, while he was still inside, recovering from Samuels's examination.

He'd been poked and prodded, twisted and pulled like a lump of bread dough. Seeing Samuels now, Brian wanted nothing more than to return the favor and mold the good-looking doctor into a much less attractive shape.

Brian had often experienced jealous feelings when he'd watched Jeff Samuels with Beth, but never more intensely than today. The man was everything a woman like Beth could want. Tall, dark and handsome, he was also a highly educated, very successful neurologist. He was sophisticated, urbane and had the debonair attitude of a man who knew his way around women. Considering the familiar arm the man had draped over Beth's shoulder and the rapt look on her face as she hung on his every word, Brian wondered—not for the first time—just how well the good doctor knew her.

Brian cursed and cursed again. If he had anything to say about it, Jeffrey Samuels was about to run up against several gigantic roadblocks where Beth was concerned. If she didn't provide them, he'd build them himself.

Fists clenched, Brian listened to her low lilting laughter mixed with Samuels's deep chuckle. The sound floated toward him on the warm summer breeze and arrived like a slap in the face. He knew damned well that he was the subject of their conversation, so why were they laughing?

If Beth was trying to convince the good doctor that the clinch he'd caught them in had inspired nothing more than her indulgent amusement, she would live to regret it. They both knew she'd been only seconds away from surrender. If Samuels hadn't come in when he had...

Another wave of laughter drifted toward him and the impact felt like a sharp kick in the stomach. "Damn it!" Brian whirled around and stalked away from the window.

One day very soon, he was going to show Elizabeth Ann Crosby that he'd probably forgotten more ways to seduce a woman than Jeff Samuels had ever learned in his urbane, sophisticated life. At the tender age of twenty, Brian had been very good in the clinches, and that was a skill a man didn't lose, even after five years. It was like riding a bike: once learned, never forgotten. All he needed was a little practice.

5

BETH'S SLENDER ARMS REACHED, pulled and reached again as she swam laps. Her body cut through the water at a speed her high school swim coach would have applauded. But unlike during a swim meet, her concentration wasn't on speed, or saving herself for that last lap, or beating the girl in the next lane. She was swimming all out. Each lap was done as if it were the final stretch.

Pushing herself to the limit, she welcomed the drain on her strength and energy. For most of the past two weeks, Beth had turned to a nightly workout in the pool, wanting to drop into bed exhausted and fall asleep instantly. Holding her temper and denying her feelings for Brian were becoming increasingly more difficult. He didn't make it easy for her, but at least she'd managed to circumvent any more heated embraces since that last night she'd caught him working out in the convalarium. However, given the work she was doing with him, it was impossible to keep any physical distance. By the end of each day, she was wound up so tightly she feared she'd explode.

Now that Brian no longer needed someone to lift him and could see to his own personal needs, Jake was gone.

Having already found another position, he'd left at the end of the second week of Brian's return to function. Beth missed the big, quiet man. She and Jake had made a good team, and she hoped they'd work together again. She'd also relied on him as a buffer between Brian and her. This past week, it had been all she could do to keep her patient at arm's length.

"Damn you, Brian Towers," Beth swore as she touched the edge of the pool, neatly tucked her body and pushed off toward the opposite end. When she surfaced, she flipped over and began a graceful backstroke at a far slower pace. She'd done it. She'd pretty well spent herself. Now all she had to do was gradually ease the tension in her muscles and let herself wind down.

Unfortunately, as her body calmed her brain went to work. She stared up into the star-studded sky, trying to concentrate on identifying the constellations, but she kept seeing images of Brian against the velvety backdrop.

"Damn your blue eyes. Damn your body for growing more gorgeous each day. Damn your persistence. Damn your intelligence. Damn your smile. Damn your voice. Damn your everything!" she chanted in rhythm with her strokes.

"Jeff warned me about this. He thinks I can handle it. Ha!" she continued, shutting her mouth just in time as she tucked and dove beneath the water for another turn.

Jeff Samuels. He was good-looking, intelligent, delightful company... and he wasn't off-limits. So why
didn't he turn her knees to jelly with a single look?

She hadn't realized how close a friend Jeff considered her until that first day after Brian had "broken
out." Though Jeff might not have seen Brian actually
kissing her, he'd guessed what had happened. While
she'd waited for him to complete his examination of
Brian, she'd readied herself for a thorough and deserved lecture on professional ethics.

However, Jeff hadn't lectured, nor in any way implied disapproval of her behavior. Instead, once he'd
given her a rundown on Brian's general physical condition and discussed the kinds of therapy Beth would
now be using, he'd draped a brotherly arm around her
shoulders and asked her to walk him to the car.

"Will you take some friendly advice?" he'd asked as
they strolled around the corner of the house.

"Sure," Beth had quickly agreed, relieved by his attitude. "I think I'm going to need all I can get."

Her hands were trembling, and she'd shoved them
into the deep pockets of her smock as she searched for
the right words. "This case was never exactly textbook, and it's taken a...a few twists since Brian has
returned to function. Maybe someone else should be
working with him now."

Jeff had stopped, stepped in front of her and gently
pulled her hands from her pockets. Holding them
firmly within his, he'd stared at them for a moment,
then smiled at her. "First, Beth Crosby, you're one of the

best, maybe the best physical therapist I know. Second, if I didn't think you were right for the job, I'd have you off it so fast your head would spin. These are capable hands I'm holding and the best Brian Towers could be placed in. Don't you forget that."

"Yes, sir," Beth had replied, pretending a jaunty smile.

"I think I can guess what Brian is feeling for you," he'd begun as he dropped her hands. Hitching a hip against the fender of his car, he gave her a thorough survey, then grinned. "You're a very attractive woman, and our patient in there is far from blind. Nor is he a eunuch. However . . ."

Jeff had paused, taken a deep breath, then looked to her as if assuring himself that he should continue. "Here comes the friendly advice. Brian's got a lot of catching up to do. Some of it's physical, some of it's emotional. I'm afraid you're going to have to deal with both. Brian's feelings for you *are* textbook. It's natural that he's formed an emotional bond to you. You'll have to find a way to keep that from interfering with your main responsibility, which is making him physically independent."

"I know, Jeff," Beth had said, shoving her hands back into her pockets and staring at her feet.

"You can do it," he'd assured her. "You're a pro." He moved away from the fender and reached for the door handle. Then he'd turned back. "And . . . uh . . . Beth. If you need a friend to talk to, I'm available."

"Thanks, Jeff." Beth had never been more sincerely grateful in her life, or needed a friend so badly.

"When's your next night off?"

"This Saturday. Why?"

"I'm not blind, either. Have dinner with me?" he'd asked, totally surprising her with the invitation. He'd evidently read the shock and the mix of emotions that must have run across her face. "Hey, just friends, seriously. We've been this route before and that's all we could come up with."

"You're right," Beth had confirmed, and had smiled up at him. "What time, Doctor?"

Beth had gone out with Jeff a couple of times since then. She had the sneaking suspicion he was taking her out as therapy for the therapist. Living on the Towers estate, so far removed from the city, Beth had been isolated from any opportunities to enjoy much of a social life. Her days and occasional nights off had been spent visiting her retired parents and married siblings, all of whom lived in the Columbus area.

In his own way, Jeff was pulling Beth back into the mainstream of life, just as Beth was trying to do for Brian. Ever so subtly, he was showing her that there were other men in the world, just as there would eventually be other women for Brian.

"Oh, Jeff." Beth sighed quietly as she floated languorously in the water. If only things were that simple. While Brian's feelings for her were no doubt immature, she knew that hers for him weren't. She was falling in love with him.

BETH WAS AT IT AGAIN. Her beautiful body, clad in a light-colored suit that disappeared in the moonlight, was cutting through the water as if all the demons of hell were chasing her. "They're chasing me, too," Brian said as he dropped the curtain and moved away from his window.

He untied his pajama bottoms and let the garment drop to the floor. Kicking the pale blue mound of cotton aside, he strode to the tall bureau across the room. "But they're going to catch us both tonight," he vowed, pulling a pair of trunks up his long legs and adjusting them over his lean hips. "Then we'll both sleep a lot better."

Within seconds, Brian was down the hall and facing the steps to the first floor. The long flight was no longer the barrier to independence it had once been, but he still had to take it slowly and grip the banister for support. Once he'd maneuvered the steps, his legs shook, and he cursed soundly when he was forced to lean against the wall for a few seconds to recover.

"Weak-kneed wimp," he condemned himself as he made his way through the darkened house.

Brian continued denouncing himself on his way out. His muscles were screaming. Beth had been right today when she'd told him he was overdoing it with the exercises. *Damn! She was always right.*

She never said "I told you so," but he saw it in her eyes when she caught him rubbing his calves in the evening. Or when he had to shuffle, one step at a time, up those blasted stairs. And when he had to break down and ask her to massage out a stubborn charley horse.

He reached for the doorknob of the convalarium, intending to take a shortcut to the pool. The knob didn't turn. She'd locked it again. He dropped his hand and stood there shaking his head, undecided whether to laugh or swear in frustration. Every night she locked her door to their adjoining bath, too. As if I'd burst through the door and attack her body!

The locked bedroom was unwarranted, but he had no one to blame but himself for the locked convalarium. She'd caught him three times in a row working out in the middle of the night, totally unsupervised. The first night he'd evaded giving a promise to stop. The second night she'd been more insistent and he'd still not quite given his word, but it had been implied. The third night? The third night had been the topper that had forced her into taking stronger measures.

He'd already gone through a session at the weight bench, pleased to press a hundred pounds without feeling much strain. He'd clocked some miles on the treadmill, then rowed a few more on the rowing machine. He'd just started in on the exercycle, when she'd walked in.

"I simply can't trust you, can I?" Beth demanded, her eyes narrow and her lips set in a firm line. She'd flipped the tension gauge to its stiffest, effectively bringing his pedaling to a halt.

Empathy had warmed her eyes and she'd shaken her head slowly. "Brian, Brian, you can't do it all in a week.

You've got to take things gradually. Don't you understand that you're overworking your heart?"

"My heart's in great shape," he'd snapped. "Your boyfriend assured me of that."

"Jeff Samuels isn't my boyfriend," Beth had returned icily, and Brian had swallowed the jealous rejoinder that came to mind. His comment had been juvenile and stupid, a mistake he'd be wise not to repeat.

"Now get off that bike and go back to bed." Assuming that he needed help, she'd wrapped an arm around his waist and started to pull him off the seat.

Draping one arm around her shoulders, Brian had docilely let her take charge until she'd maneuvered him to a standing position on the floor. Then he'd curled his other arm around her waist and folded her close. "How's your heart, Beth?" he'd asked as he lowered his head. "Does it accelerate for me as mine does for you?" Then he'd kissed her.

He'd run his tongue along the line of her lips, tasted their nectar, then hungered for more. When she'd whimpered a protest, he'd taken advantage and plunged his tongue inside. Gathering her closer, he'd continued the seduction of her mouth.

Lord, she'd felt so good, so right. With only the thin layers of their nightclothes between them, he'd had a glimpse of what it would be like when their bodies fit together in a more intimate lovers' embrace.

Her breasts pressed against his chest, he'd felt the aroused peaks he'd so wanted to kiss. He'd run his hands down her back. He'd inventoried every line, indentation and curve before he'd covered her bottom with his hands and lifted her higher and tighter against him. He'd been throbbing with need for her and had barely restrained himself from tearing away what little separated them and taking her there on the floor.

"I love you," he'd murmured against the curve of her neck and shoulder. "Come up to bed with me. I need you so."

"Brian." She'd breathed his name on a long sigh and he'd never wanted all his strength back so badly. If only he could have swept her into his arms, carried her up the stairs and taken her to his bed. But he hadn't been able to, and even if he had, Beth wouldn't have allowed it.

"No, Brian!" Her tone had been sharp, but her voice had shaken and he'd known she'd been just as affected as he.

"I'm sorry this happened," she'd said, backing away from him. Her eyes had been wide and dark. A visible tremor had rippled through her body and she'd wrapped her arms protectively around herself. "I shouldn't have let things go this far. I'll help you up those stairs and that's all!"

Since that night, she'd locked the convalarium after every afternoon session. He'd often wondered whether it was really to prevent him from using the equipment without her supervision or to prevent herself from ending up in his bed. A little of both, he decided as he drew closer to his destination.

Standing at the sliding glass door that opened onto the patio beside the pool, Brian hesitated. He waited until she'd touched the opposite end and made her turn. Her gaze was directed at the receding pool edge as she backstroked toward him; she wouldn't see him slip into the water.

If his guess was right, the last person she wanted to share that pool with was him. He was sure she was seeking release from the same tension he was suffering. Swimming laps wasn't the solution any more than his cold showers had been.

Luckily her pace had slowed drastically. She was no longer streaking across the pool, but floating for long intervals between slow languid strokes. He was about to slide soundlessly into the water, when he heard her say, "Jeff."

Jeff! It was hard enough to control his jealousy whenever she danced out of the house on the good doctor's arm. It was next to impossible to tolerate her sighing the quack's name within his hearing!

Catching his bellow of outrage before it broke the serenity of the summer night, Brian lowered himself into the water. It wasn't nearly cold enough to cool his temper. He slammed his feet against the tiled wall and pushed off with all his strength.

As he cut through the water, he was careful to keep his body beneath the surface, preventing any sound from alerting Beth. He wanted to rid himself of his jealousy before revealing his presence, knowing she would consider such a display another sign of his supposed immaturity.

BETH FELT MOTION. Treading water, she turned around, looking for the cause of the vibrations. A dark shape beneath the surface was gliding toward her. Since the only one at home this evening was Brian, she knew who it was. Before she could spin around and head for the side, his head emerged less than a foot from hers.

"Hi. Don't you know it's unsafe to swim alone?" he asked guilelessly, his legs brushing against hers as they faced each other.

Beth moved backward, the touch of his body negating all the good her workout had accomplished. "What are you doing here? You're supposed to be asleep."

"So are you," he drawled as he followed her retreat, purposely ignoring her attempt to keep some distance between them. "You've been out here all by yourself night after night and I finally decided to join you. I know why you're here, Beth."

"Oh, really?" She kept treading backward, but was unable to evade him. He was pacing his advance to the speed of her retreat.

There was just enough light from the moon and the lamps at the pool's edge for her to read his eyes. They weren't reflecting the fear she was certain was showing in hers. He was reaching into her, pulling at her every sense, just as he'd been doing all day.

Intuiting some new purpose in him, she'd escaped early to her room and tried to concentrate on a novel.

Giving it up, she'd waited until she was sure Brian would be asleep before coming outside. She should have stayed in her room.

"Brian . . ." Beth warned, cursing herself for not having guessed his intentions before this. "This is *my* time. I'm not here as your twenty-four-hour therapist."

"I'm counting on that. I don't need a therapist. Right now we're just a man and a woman who have something very special between them."

Beth's shoulders bumped against the edge of the pool. Brian reached around her and placed an arm on either side of her. She was trapped. Her only defense now was words. "Brian, don't do this. Don't use me to gratify some macho need to establish your masculinity."

"You can't think that's what I'm doing," he retorted quickly, but Beth knew her words had hurt him. She had seen the way his jaw had tightened, his eyes had dulled, and she hurt for him. Yet she was sure she was right. Out of self-preservation she had to cling to that theory.

"What else can I think? You come out here, jump in the pool with me and immediately start coming on to me? You don't want me, Brian. I'm available, and you're right, there is something special between us. But it's not love—"

"At least you'll admit there's something," he interrupted. "But you're wrong about the macho thing. I never needed a woman to establish my masculinity. It's been five years, but I haven't changed that much."

Beth could believe him. She was sure Brian had probably had a maturity and self-confidence at twenty that some men didn't gain before they were thirty, if ever. He'd had everything. Soon he would have it again.

"Beth." He tilted his head to one side and smiled a smile that would have warmed the coldest heart. "I know you. Almost as well as you know yourself. And you know me. We've had six months of togetherness.

"While I was locked in, all I could do was communicate with my eyes and fight my body's reaction to you. I've been wanting you for months and thought I'd never be able to do anything about it. Can you imagine the kinds of fantasies I've had about what I'd do if I was ever able to move?"

"That's what they are—fantasies," she maintained, trying to resist his smile, his voice, the desire in his eyes.

"They *were* fantasies, Beth," he agreed as he dipped his head and licked a water droplet from her bare shoulder. "Now they can be realities. Just like the fantasies you've had about me."

"I haven't had any fantasies about you," she denied vehemently, shrinking against the tiles as Brian continued to sip the moisture from her shoulders. Breathing rapidly, she laid her hands against his chest, wanting to push him away. Her brain's directive wasn't received. Instead of pushing, her palms curved to the contours of his muscles, the muscles she'd worked to maintain and then to rebuild. She'd done too good a job, she thought irrationally.

"You've had fantasies," he murmured against her neck. "Not as long as I've had them. But toward the end, long after we'd established communication, sometimes you'd let down your guard and your eyes would get all dreamy, soft, warm. You didn't kiss me that first time just to shock me and get my attention."

Beth turned her head to evade his lips. "That was an impulsive whim."

"Impulsive, maybe." Undeterred, he nibbled along her neck and toward her ear. "Thank God you did it."

"Brian, that kiss didn't bring you out. I've told you before. I don't have magic kisses." *But you do*, she wanted to declare.

"Yes, you do, my love," he said softly as he framed her face between his hands. "They're magic, all right." He kissed the corners of her mouth. "Magic."

His lips captured hers with a tenderly delivered whisper of her name. He persuaded and coaxed by gently brushing his lips across hers. It was tantalizing and irresistible.

Unable to help herself, Beth responded; the magic was all his. She was defeated, caught up in the spell that was Brian. She openly invited the intimacy of his tongue's invasion.

The kiss had a dreamy quality that sent a soul-reaching message. Beth drank of the sweetness of Brian's mouth as he sipped at hers. In seconds, all thought of protest fled.

Their minds on nothing but the delights of each other, they stopped treading water and slowly sank beneath the surface. Enclosed in liquid warmth, they were cushioned from the world, nothing existed beyond the wonder of their embrace.

Finally the need for air drove them toward the surface.

"Hold on to me." With one arm around Beth's waist, Brian sidestroked toward the shallow end of the pool.

Seconds later, he had righted himself, scooping Beth up against his chest. Fearing a protest, he silenced her with a deep kiss while carrying her up the steps to the patio. Though he felt as strong as he had once been, he was thankful the double-width chaise where he'd lain so many times was close by. He didn't want to chance a sudden attack of weak knees. Not now. Not when he held the woman he loved in his arms.

He followed her down to the cushions, lying half over and half off her. "Beth, Beth. You are so incredibly beautiful." He punctuated his words with kisses starting at her throat and trailing downward.

At the gentle swell of her breasts he stopped. Reaching for her nape, he undid the halter fastening of her suit.

Beth had a fleeting thought that Brian obviously had plenty of experience removing women's clothing, but his kiss erased all logic and reason. His tongue engaged hers in a rhythmic dance that left them both gasping, and then, raising himself above her, he peeled the suit down to her waist to gaze at her moon-silvered body. "Beautiful."

Gently and reverently, he outlined the circle of her breast with his hand, skimming across her sensitive, swollen nipple. Finally he lowered his head and his lips soothed the rosy peak. Almost mindless with the need to feel his lips on her body, Beth drove her hands into his thick hair and pressed his head closer.

"So sweet, so silky," he murmured as he adored her. "I knew you would be like this. I want you Beth. All of you. Tonight." He slid his palm down her side, curled it over her hip, then moved it to her bared midriff. His fingers slipped beneath the wet fabric bunched at her waist. He caressed her abdomen and dipped farther.

Beth's caution hung by so slender a thread, she knew she couldn't stop Brian if he wanted to make love to her. If he touched her now, where the heart of her desire throbbed for him, she would be gone. "Brian, help me," she said so softly he barely heard her. "Please help me."

Something in her voice warned him that she wasn't urging him on. Though her body was quivering and writhing beneath him, obviously as aroused as his, a part of her wasn't with him. "Beth?" He lifted his head and gazed at her tortured features, recognizing the signs of anguish. "I want to love you."

"I know that, Brian," Beth said shakily. "And I can't stop you."

Feeling as if he were violating her, Brian moved his hands, placing them on either side of her head. He dropped a soft kiss on her forehead, then heaved himself over to lie beside her. He gave himself the time to take a few calming breaths and bring the demands of his body under his mind's control. "Are you saying you don't want me?"

"No."

Totally confused, Brian rolled to his side. Leaning over her, he saw anxiety and something else in her eyes. He saw desire. It was unmistakable, but he couldn't ignore the reservations that shadowed it.

"Beth, I love you," he said, praying those three simple words would convey all that he was feeling. "I'd never hurt you. I—" Brian stopped himself. Even to his own ears, he sounded like a pleading kid.

"I'm only human and you're a handsome and very desirable man," Beth began, knowing any reference to ethics would infuriate him. Besides, ethics wasn't the only issue here. Even though her ardor had cooled, she knew it would take only one more kiss to send her spinning off to a sensual world from which there would be no return. "We've been through so much together, but this isn't real, Brian."

"It's real, babe," Brian disagreed on an anguished moan. He felt as if he were going to burst with need for her. He settled himself between her thighs and pressed his hardened groin into her softness.

Beth caught her breath, squeezed her eyes shut and tried valiantly to shrink away from him, but couldn't. "You don't play fair."

He dropped a short, quick kiss on her lips. "You know what they say, 'All's fair in love and war,'" he told her blithely, and smiled down at her. His smile didn't last more than a second when he read her expression.

Fear overshadowed her desire and he knew he couldn't go through with this. He could have her, but he would have only her body. Being immersed and enclosed in her soft warmth was tempting, but he couldn't force her.

"You don't play fair, either, sweetheart," he finally said, pulling up her suit to cover her before he changed his mind. "What we're feeling is real, but evidently it's too soon for you to realize that. I've waited this long. I guess I can wait a little longer."

"Thank you, Brian," Beth said, and raised a trembling hand to his cheek.

He turned his face and kissed her palm. "You can thank me by letting me hold you a little longer, but don't move. Whatever you do don't move, or my promise is void."

Brian swept his arms beneath her, while Beth wrapped hers around his shoulders. He rested his head on her breast. Unconsciously she traced circles with her palms over his back. Neither of them moved for a long time, until Beth sensed the tension ease from his body. Brian welcomed the soothing. The almost maternal quality in her touch he hated.

6

BETH STARED INCREDULOUSLY at the huge bay gelding pawing the gravel drive and at the man intending to ride him. "It's only two days before your mother's party, Brian. Everyone's looking forward to seeing you up and about. Why try something this risky now?"

She couldn't believe Brian actually meant to take on such a mean-looking beast, but obviously he was serious. Dressed in a dark shirt, tan jodhpurs and knee-high, brown leather boots, he looked like a man on his way to a polo match instead of one who hadn't been anywhere near a horse in five years.

"Can't you at least start out on something smaller than this monster?"

"Centaur is my horse. I'll ride him." Sliding the reins through his gloved hand, Brian mounted the animal in one fluid movement. "I've been riding all my life, Beth. Stop worrying. There's no risk."

Beth disagreed violently, though she didn't want to get into another match of wills with him. After six weeks of such confrontations, she was well aware how little chance there was of her winning this round. Even so, she had to try. He might look totally recovered, but he had yet to acquire the strength necessary to control such a mammoth animal. "What happens if he gets away from you? Or if you fall off?"

"I'll have to walk home," Brian replied calmly as he adjusted his long legs in the stirrups. Glancing down at her, he noted her horrified expression and laughed. "I'm getting real good at walking, or hadn't you noticed?"

Beth strove hard to keep her temper and match his unruffled tone. "Walking a mile on even ground isn't quite the same as going up and down hills covered with trees and underbrush. And if you're hurt, it could be hours before anyone finds you. I've got three days left here, Brian. I'd rather you didn't break your fool neck until after I've gone."

His exasperated look didn't reveal half the frustration he felt whenever he considered her leaving. *Three days*, he thought bleakly. He only had three short days to make her believe that he loved her and to make her admit that she loved him, too. So far, nothing he'd done had helped his cause. He needed to be alone for a few hours to rethink his strategy, though he could hardly tell her that. "I'm not going to break my neck."

Seeing the stubborn set of his chin, Beth made a suggestion without considering the consequences. "Then let me come with you." She stepped forward and placed her hand on his leg as a gesture of appeal. She felt the muscle retract beneath her palm, but she still thought it her duty to be with him if he ended up having to pay for his own stupidity.

She refused to step out of his path. "Please, Brian," she said with a long-suffering sigh. "Show some sense for a change."

Brian had just about had it with the attitude she'd adopted toward him and her insulting estimation of his maturity. She used both as a shield to keep him at arm's length and he hated it. In snug-fitting jeans and a soft, clingy tank top, she didn't look like his mother, but she sure as hell acted like her.

"Taking you with me would defeat the whole purpose of this ride," he informed her. "I don't need a nursemaid and that's what you've become. I'd risk more than my neck to escape your harping, and I don't give a damn if that makes any sense to you or not."

Beth snatched her hand from his leg as if burned. Turning on her heel, she started toward the house. "Fine," she flung out over her shoulder, blinking back the tears of hurt that smarted in her eyes. "Go ahead. Behave like an idiot and get yourself killed. I'm through worrying about you."

The next thing Beth knew, she was being yanked off her feet. For several seconds she acted purely on instinct, grabbing for whatever there was to grab, which turned out to be Brian's arm. Her own arm felt as if it were being pulled from the socket as she was swung up in the air. Scissoring her legs, she landed half on and half off the horse's rump.

Terror-stricken, she righted herself as best she could. She had never been on a horse this size in her life, never ridden anything more spirited than the plodding ponies that walked around in a ring at the state fair. Her offer to accompany him had been prompted by desperation, not because she had any qualifications as a horsewoman.

"Let me down!" she shouted in his ear, her fingers clutching handfuls of his shirt on either side of his waist as she fought for balance. "Damn you, Brian! I mean it. Let me down." But even as she stated her demands, her thighs clamped like a vice around his buttocks and hips.

"You wanted to come, so now you're coming," Brian mocked. "Better hang on tight, mother hen."

He started off at a slow canter, giving her time to adjust to being up in the saddle, but as soon as he felt her breasts pressed hard against his back and her arms tight around his waist, he gave Centaur his head. The huge bay took off like a Lear jet, picking up speed with every length of the white rail fence that ran parallel to the drive.

Brian felt the wind whipping his face and flowing through his hair. He took a deep breath, savoring the speed and the power that coursed beneath him. With every pounding stride of the horse, his exhilaration increased. He lifted his face to the wind and got high on the glorious sense of challenge and absolute freedom that came from riding such a magnificent creature. Lord, how he had missed this feeling of liberation. How he loved it!

Forgetting all about the breathless woman clinging to his back like a limpet, he let out a joyous whoop and charged for the open fields where nothing could hamper Centaur's high-spirited flight. The fragrance of wildflowers and cut grass rose to meet him as they galloped across a seemingly endless stretch of freshly mown hay. As far as the eye could see was Towers land, acres and acres of rolling hills, grassy meadows and lush forests in the full bloom of summer.

Behind him was the sprawling main house, the pool and tennis court, a five-car garage and the stables, but spread out before him was the real wealth of the family. Out there were the green fields of growing crops, the pride of their breeding stock and the land, the ever bountiful, ever present land. It had been cleared by his great-grandfather, nourished by his grandfather, preserved by his father, and was loved by him.

Wanting to see everything at once, Brian raced Centaur past the dairy cattle and horses grazing in nearby pastures, past the stately stands of chestnut and oak and the thick grove where he'd spent so many hours in boyhood adventure. He rode past the outbuildings that housed all the modern machinery that made the farm prosper, along freshly painted fences and gurgling brooks.

Finally he came to a stop at the last fence surrounding Towers property. He didn't need to go any farther. By some miracle, this unique sense of belonging, being one with the earth and all growing things had been given back to him. God willing, he'd never have to forfeit it again.

As soon as he'd ordered Centaur to a halt, Brian became aware of the feminine arms wrapped around his waist and the rapid heartbeat of their owner. Throughout the ride, she'd been one with him, too, at least in his mind. However, though they had stopped, she was still hanging on to him for all she was worth. Her nose was pressed between his shoulder blades, her chin digging into his back, and he realized that she didn't share his bliss.

Brian attempted to swivel around in the saddle, but Beth wouldn't loosen her grasp. Only then did he truly comprehend that she was too frightened to move. "Beth." He spoke her name softly, soothingly. "It's okay. We're stopped. You can let go now."

All he received for that effort was a ragged sigh and an agonized gulp. Unwilling to add insult to injury, Brian still ended up having to pry her fingers apart in order to break her hold on him. He dismounted immediately, then reached up for her. As gently as possible, he set her back on her feet, gripping her arms until he was sure her quaking legs would keep her upright.

Seeing the wet trails of tears that stained her cheeks and the quivering of her full bottom lip, he was overcome by remorse. "Beth, I'm sorry. I had no idea you'd react like this. Please forgive me."

Wanting to kick himself for his stupidity and selfishness, Brian watched as she slowly regained control. First her legs stopped trembling, then her fingers unclenched and finally she opened her eyes. His first indication that her subsequent response to panic was hysterical anger came with the vitriolic shriek that denigrated his heritage. The next was the painful throbbing of his big toe as her shoe came down on it. Then she started swinging.

He knew she'd never forgive herself if she managed to land a blow, so he ducked beneath a lethal right hook and tackled her. He tried very hard not to hurt her as he tumbled her to the short, spiky grass.

"Calm down!" he pleaded with the completely outraged female squirming beneath him.

"Bastard!" She repeated her new name for him, thrusting out her chin as she glared up at him with blazing dark eyes. "I'll never forgive you for this. Never!"

"Which this?" Brian asked, beginning to pant with the strain of keeping her still. "Scaring the life out of you with that mad gallop on Centaur or taking you down with a flying tackle?"

"Take your pick," Beth raged, though she could feel the effects of adrenaline fading away, leaving only exhaustion. A second later she went limp, all the fight gone out of her. "You're hurting me."

"Then we're even," Brian muttered. He released her wrists, rolled off her and sat up.

Still stretched out on her back and breathing heavily, Beth gazed up at his crestfallen expression. His impossible blue eyes looked wounded. His head dropped into his hands as he pulled up his knees, and his shoulders heaved in a despondent shrug. If it was possible for a grown man to pout, he was pouting.

Beth hadn't really meant to cause him pain. She sat up, feeling a stab of guilt. It was just that she'd been so scared.

She still hadn't said anything, conciliatory or otherwise, by the time Brian stood up and hobbled over to the gelding. "You're limping," she noted, unable to keep the worry from her tone.

"It's my natural reaction to having my foot stamped on," Brian commented as he grabbed hold of Centaur's reins. His expression was discouraging as he faced her again, his eyes on the ground. "Come on. I'll walk you back to the house."

"Take your boot off and let me look at it."

"What?" His eyes shot to her face, studying features that were as pale as his own, but also soft with concern. Even after what he'd just done to her, she felt the need to come to his aid. When she got to her feet and walked over to him, urging him to sit down so she could pull off his boot, a great tide of hopelessness washed over him.

Suddenly everything seemed clear, painfully, gut-wrenchingly clear. Beth would always feel this way about him, always see him as an overly rambunctious patient needing motherly care, an emotionally backward man who refused to accept his own limitations.

Brian knew he had no choice but to accept this particular limitation. He saw now, that no matter how much he loved her, Beth Crosby was off-limits to him and always would be. There was nothing he could do or say to change that. She couldn't see him as a rational, mature man, and he couldn't share his life with a woman who felt that way about him.

The acknowledgment hit him with the force of a ten-ton weight crashing down on his chest; the acceptance made him feel even worse. He sank down on the ground, saying nothing as Beth's fingers closed around his heel and lifted his foot.

Unaware of the bitter defeat in his eyes, she threw his boot on the ground and peeled off his sock. "Where does it hurt?"

"All over," he whispered, but at her confused look, pointed to his injured toe. "It's nothing, Beth. When we get home, I'll soak it in a bucket of water and that will be that."

He gritted his teeth as she made up her mind whether to accept his self-diagnosis and course of treatment. Now, even more than when he'd first gotten up on Centaur's back, he yearned to be alone. After taking Beth back to the house, he'd go off somewhere and lick his wounds. Maybe then he'd be able to attend his mother's party without making a fool of himself, and the day after that, say goodbye to Beth without letting her see the gaping wounds she'd left in his soul.

Even now he was dying to touch her, the ache inside him so great it hurt to breathe. He wanted her naked. He wanted to be inside her more badly than he'd ever wanted anything…except her respect. If he didn't have that, making love to her would kill him. Until today, he thought he might chance it.

"I see a creek over there on the other side of the fence," Beth announced, sitting back on her heels. She lifted the heavy, honey-and-chocolate ponytail off her neck, unaware that in doing so, her breasts shifted provocatively. "Why don't we soak our feet in the water before we go back. I don't know about you, but I'm awfully hot."

"Good idea." Brian dragged his eyes away from her, clenching his fists to prevent his treacherous fingers from having what they wanted.

At any other time, Beth realized, Brian would have pounced on the sexual implications of her statement "I'm hot." The fact that he hadn't, acquiescing meekly to her suggestion, gave Beth pause. Maybe his toe wasn't just bruised but broken, and he really was in a lot of pain.

"Let me help you," she said as he stood up and started walking toward the fence.

Her touch on his arm set off something she could never have expected and he couldn't prevent. He jerked away, his voice harsh with pain as he snarled, "For God's sake! Leave me alone. Don't you know I can't stand having you touch me?"

At the shattered look on her face, he stripped away another layer of his soul. "I love you, Beth, with all my heart."

Beth didn't know what to say. She loved him, too, but she still couldn't trust that his feelings would last or even if they were real. Even so, she had never heard

such desolation in any man's voice. "Brian...I don't...
You can't— "

"I'm afraid I can even if you don't," he interrupted
harshly, stepping back as she stepped forward. "Please.
If you care at all, then leave me with some self-respect.
Otherwise I won't be responsible for what happens."

As soon as the words had left his mouth, he began
walking away. At the fence, he vaulted over the top rail,
then continued a few more feet before finally throwing
himself down on the creek bank. He pulled off his remaining boot and thrust his feet in the cool water.

Beth took her time following him, trying to decide
how best to approach him again. She couldn't leave him
alone as he'd requested, no matter what the consequences. She loved him. And Brian Towers had suffered more in five years than most people endured in a
lifetime, and she couldn't bear to think that she was the
cause of additional pain.

When she reached the bank, Beth sat down on the
grass a few feet from him. Saying nothing, she removed her shoes and socks. The cool water soothed her
hot feet, but did nothing to ease her tumultuous state
of mind. Considering the results, all the arguments she
had used to prevent herself from becoming seriously
involved with Brian—and he with her—seemed not
only futile but unnecessarily cruel.

It had to be faced—she was involved, deeply involved. The least she could do was acknowledge Brian's
feelings, whether or not they were grounded in reality.
"I do care about you, Brian. I care very much."

Her words fell into silence. Brian didn't even glance up and he didn't move. Beth forced herself to look at him, biting her lip when she saw his closed eyes. He had shut down, drawn all the pain into himself, just as he had when he'd been locked in.

"If I didn't care, Brian, if I didn't love you, I wouldn't try so hard to keep you at a distance. You've missed out on so much. Very soon you'll be taking up where you left off five years ago, and you may find there's no place in that life for me. I could be a reminder of a time you'd rather forget. Giving in to my feelings for you before you discover what's waiting out there wouldn't be fair to either one of us." Beth searched his face for a response, but there was none.

She scooted across the grass and took hold of his hand. Bringing his palm to her breast, she pleaded, "Please listen to me, Brian. Please don't shut me out."

Beth watched as he drew in his breath, opened his eyes for a second, then closed them again. She watched the pulse beating at his temple...once...twice... three times. Not realizing that she was doing it, she counted to ten, and his lashes lifted. She responded to the familiar signal automatically, forgetting that he no longer had to communicate with his eyes.

"I'm not trying to win anything, Brian," she insisted. "I'm trying to make you understand why we can't be together. As your friend, making love with you now would be the worst possible thing I could do. Don't you see how wrong it would be?"

Blink. *No.* Brian didn't see. He would never see why it was wrong for two people who loved each other to make love. As far as he was concerned, his feelings for her were beautiful, strong and good. Whatever the future, he would always feel that way. As she did, he cherished their friendship, the special link between them. But as precious as that was, he needed more.

Beth looked into the deep blue eyes staring down at her, and understood that she should have taken herself off the case the moment Brian had returned to function. She could read the self-doubt and vulnerability in his eyes and knew that she alone had put it there.

She wanted to reach out and stroke his forehead to soothe his fears away, but knew he would view the action as another acknowledgment of her maternal feelings toward him, feelings he rejected. Neither could she kiss him with passion as she longed to do, for then he would feel morally bound to her at a time when he most needed to be free. "Knowing how I felt about you, Brian, I should have realized that by staying on, I was only compounding the problem. I think it would be best if I left here today. I . . . I never meant to hurt you like this."

Her voice faltered on a sob and the last few words came out close to a whisper. "I'm so sorry."

Beth was caught in the snare of her own emotions, unable to move as tears overwhelmed her. She felt herself drawn against a solid male chest, felt Brian's arms encircling her, comforting her, but she couldn't stop crying. After all the days and nights of caring for him, loving him, the knowledge that she'd hurt him tore into her like a sharp knife.

"Don't be sorry for loving me, Beth," Brian murmured achingly, framing her face in his hands. "I'll never be sorry for loving you. Never!"

When words didn't erase the pain he saw in her eyes, he acted on instinct. He lowered his head and kissed the tears from her lips. He took the sob that tore from her throat into his own mouth, trying desperately to take the hurting, as well. His hands trembled on her face, then fell to her waist as he pulled her against him, wanting to absorb her anguish into himself.

Moments or hours later, Beth was no longer cradled in his arms but lying beneath him. Brian kissed her over and over again, until it was suddenly too late for either of them to pull back. Beth's body reacted helplessly to the responsive tremors she felt in his and she could no more stop the yielding than hold back time.

From the very beginning of their relationship, they had shared a unique affinity. Like the powerful force in nature that combines atoms and keeps them combined, Brian and Beth were drawn to each other, yearning to be one. Every nerve, every cell in every muscle and bone cried out for the mating and within seconds this elemental need overcame all else.

Neither of them knew when or how the barriers of clothing were removed, and neither cared. It wouldn't have surprised them if the material had disintegrated through spontaneous combustion, consumed by the fire that raged within them. Then, as naked flesh met naked flesh, the flames burned even higher and hotter.

Beth moaned as Brian's hands moved over her, touching her in all the ways she'd dreamed of being touched by him. She felt worshipped and adored, overwhelmed by the shattering hunger she sensed in him and the incredible restraint he showed by placing her pleasure ahead of his own. She returned his generosity in equal measure.

Tasting and touching, she was totally uninhibited in her exploration of his body. He was glorious and she in her glory when they finally came together. With shaking urgency, he entered her, watching her as he moved and waiting until she was ready to match the wild rhythm he longed to set.

"Brian." She breathed his name, a whisper of sound that mixed with his own awed pronouncement. "Beth." And then the wildness took over, escalating dizzily with heat and excitement until they were devoured by unrestrainable passion.

They lay shaking in the aftermath, awestruck and dazed. The summer sun still shone down upon them, the rippling water in the creek continued to flow and the trees over their heads hadn't moved, but to them, everything had changed and become that much more beautiful.

Beth opened her eyes and the first thing she saw was a tiny wildflower nestled in the grass. A lovely, radiant pink, its petals appeared so fragile and delicate that the slightest breeze could shred them.

As her rational mind began working again, Beth identified with the flower. She felt lovely, radiant, but also on the verge of being stripped of all that made her so. Brian was still within her, a part of her, but soon he would have to withdraw from her and she from him.

For a few wondrous moments she had bloomed in his arms, as brilliantly as the wildflower now bloomed in the grasses. Like the flower, she had reached the point of ultimate vibrancy and life, the peak of her feminine beauty. But the moment had passed, and with the passing came withering truth.

She reached out for the flower and gently plucked it. Careful not to harm the soft petals, she enclosed it in her hand as a memento. Whenever she looked back, the flower would remind her of this time in the sun, a time of shared wonder and natural harmony with the man she loved.

As for now, it was time to say goodbye.

7

"MAKE A FIST for me, Katie," Beth encouraged and with an approving smile rewarded the bright-eyed little girl when she curled her pudgy fingers into her palm. "That's it. Now can you do that with your other hand?"

It took far more effort, but the five-year-old was finally able to tighten the fingers of her left hand into a fist. "I'm proud of you, Katie. You're a very hard worker," Beth enthused, truly awed by the child's quick recovery from the virulent disease that had attacked her nervous system.

Less than one month ago, Katie Buchanan had been completely paralyzed from the neck down, unable to breathe on her own. Now she was not only off the respirator, but she was able to talk, stand, even walk a few steps without assistance. With a few more weeks of physical therapy, Beth knew that Katie would have regained enough mobility to leave as an outpatient. A short while after that, the child would require no further treatment.

Beth wished some of her other patients would progress at such a rapid rate. In the year since she'd accepted this position at the renowned Shelton Convalescent Center, she'd worked with dozens of neurological patients. None of them had made the kind of progress Katie had.

After Brian's spectacular recovery, Beth no longer doubted that miracles could happen. Even so, she knew that to expect such an occurrence in every case would be doing a terrible disservice to those people who had to be taught to live with a permanent disability.

"Aren't I done yet?" Katie inquired impatiently as Beth watched her wiggle her pink toes. "Roxie's coming."

"So soon?" Beth glanced at her watch. She was amazed that two hours had gone by since she'd begun her morning session with Katie. It was past eleven o'clock. Noting the relieved expression on her pint-sized patient's face, she teased, "Don't tell me you'd rather go swimming than do some more leg exercises."

The child nodded eagerly. "Swimming's more fun."

Beth laughed. "So I've heard."

"Your chariot awaits, milady," Roxanne Valentine, a woman who looked like a short, plump female version of Huckleberry Finn, gestured grandly to the unoccupied seat of the wheelchair thrust out in front of her. "Are you ready to splash around in the pool?"

"I sure am," Katie confirmed with a giggle.

A mother of five, Roxie adored children and had a natural rapport with them that Beth envied. She wore a perpetual smile and was looked on as a ray of sunshine by both patients and staff. "Are you taking a break soon, Roxie?" Beth asked, hoping to share a cup of coffee with someone who never failed to put her in a good mood.

"I'll be through here in a few minutes," Roxie said.

With Beth's assistance Katie was quickly installed in the chair. Then Roxie pronounced with a flourish, "Here we go. Vroom!"

Pushing the wheelchair toward the double doors that led to the indoor pool, she called back, "Beth, I'll meet you in the cafeteria as soon as I drop off Katie with Betty Lou. And check out the morning newspaper. I left it folded on the back table. There's a blip in there about your pride and joy. He's really becoming the man about town."

As soon as she reached the cafeteria, Beth grabbed up the paper. Less than a minute later, it was deposited in the trash. Beth was glad she'd been alone when she'd read the small article about Brian and seen the accompanying picture. Roxie would have been astonished by her angry reaction.

Assuming her interest in Brian Towers was due to the part Beth had played in his recovery, Roxie hadn't questioned Beth's motives for keeping track of him. Thinking she was doing Beth a favor, she pointed out every reference made to him in the papers, cut out articles and pictures. Roxie would never understand why Beth ripped this one to shreds.

Beth would have liked to tell her well-meaning friend that she no longer wanted Brian's name mentioned in her presence, let alone have to look at pictures. But then she'd have to explain why. After what she'd seen in the paper today, she felt enough of a fool as it was. She, not her ex-patient, was the foolish victim of misplaced affection, a real textbook case.

Over the past year, Beth had diligently gathered together a sizable collection of clippings on Brian and she had devoured every word in them. The pictures she'd saved so religiously had depicted his continued physical progress, his amazing vitality and undaunted spirit. Until today, she had thought she'd never tire of looking at them. Now she couldn't wait to get home to throw all those reminders away.

She had felt considerable pride when she'd read the first human interest story done on him last fall, wherein he'd mentioned the valiant physical therapist who had never let him lose faith in himself or doubt his chances to regain total function. That article had so impressed the administration at the Shelton Convalescent Center that she'd had no trouble landing a job at the extended care facility.

She had been overjoyed when six months later she'd read that he'd obtained his degree in business and that he had started work as a junior executive in the family company. Ensuing articles had referred to his volunteer work with other victims of coma and the charitable efforts he and his family had undertaken in the community.

Recently the Shelton Center had received a generous donation from the Towers Foundation to be used for the purchase of the most modern therapeutic equipment available. Even knowing that her employment at the center had had nothing to do with the gift, Beth couldn't help but be pleased. It made her feel good to know that the Towerses' interest in neurological disorders hadn't ceased with Brian's recovery.

Pride and joy—she had experienced both emotions in the past twelve months, but she'd also endured unceasing loneliness. She had long since conceded that she loved Brian and always would. A day didn't pass that she didn't think of him, long for him, miss him.

She derived a good deal of satisfaction from the knowledge that he was accomplishing everything she had ever wanted for him. He was operating successfully in the mainstream of society. No matter what, she would always be happy about that. On the other hand, she'd hoped that he wouldn't be able to forget her any more than she was able to forget him.

She'd dreamed of the day when he'd come to her and announce that his feelings for her hadn't changed. He would say that he'd made the most of the opportunity she'd given him to test his feelings, and that his love for her had not only endured but grown stronger. As time went on, however, and he made no effort to contact her, Beth had been forced to accept the possibility that Brian had forgotten her.

The shredded picture in the trash was tangible proof that he had. Through the open door of a limousine, the photographer had captured Brian and a stunning blonde in a passionate clinch. The accompanying article had described Brian Towers and Melinda Graham, a local newscaster, as a "golden couple" who had shined at the regional Emmy Awards banquet. Melinda had won an award for co-anchoring the six o'clock news and her handsome escort deserved one for winning his fight back to good health. The writer had wished them both well and hinted that their association might become permanent.

Beth closed her eyes. *Permanent.* She was painfully familiar with the meaning of the word. Her love for Brian was permanent—everlasting without change. The antonym of *permanent* was *fleeting*, an apt description of Brian's love for her.

All her doubts concerning a future with him had been confirmed. She'd been right to say goodbye when she had, to leave before he felt any obligation for the way she felt about him. Now, he could go to Melinda Graham with a clear conscience.

Being right gave Beth no satisfaction at all. She was overwhelmed by jealousy. Her altruistic gesture had been rewarded by losing Brian to another woman. Placing his needs first, she had urged him to explore other relationships, and to her dismay, he was doing just that.

"Great-looking couple aren't they?" Roxie joined her at the table. "The perfect ending for the case of Brian Towers."

"The perfect ending," Beth repeated, but couldn't bring herself to smile.

TWO WEEKS LATER, Beth sat in the cafeteria with all the other employees of the Shelton Center. The work day was over and Forrest Gallagher, the center's administrator was about to begin what Roxie called his annual "One for the Gipper" speech. The first Saturday in September each year, the center held a charity auction to raise funds from the private sector. In addition to items donated by local businessmen, members of the staff were expected to contribute an hour or more of service to the highest bidder.

"Oh-oh," Roxie groaned. "This bodes ill. Gallagher's wearing his best teddy bear smile. We're all doomed."

"He does look a bit like a teddy bear," Beth agreed, noting the man's snappy dark eyes, shaggy head of brown hair and robust form. "Maybe that's why I always have this urge to hug him."

"Just remember that bears are carnivores," Roxie advised.

Betty Lou Johnson, the most senior physical therapist in the group added her two cents' worth. "As the new kid on the block, I'm warning you, Beth, put in for an ounce and our fearless leader will take a pound."

"Of flesh," Roxie cautioned. "Last year I said I'd wash cars. I'm still suffering from dishpan hands."

"Don't listen to them, Beth," Jeff Samuels inserted as he took the last empty chair at their table. "I washed cars, too, and I'm none the worse for wear."

"I washed. You wiped," Roxie recalled with an affronted expression.

"Well, these *are* the hands of an expert surgeon," Jeff reminded her, his pompous tone belied by an engaging grin. Lifting both hands, he wiggled his fingers. "I can't afford to take too many chances with these babies."

"Why didn't someone tell me he'd switched from neurology to neurosurgery?" Beth inquired of the group. "When did this happen?"

"Actually, it happens every year right before auction time," Jeff admitted, tongue in cheek. "Forrest goes easy on surgeons. When they tell him they won't wrestle Hulk Hogan, type two thousand letters for the League of Women Voters or build a domed stadium, he suggests something less tiring, like mowing lawns at Sciota Country Club or washing all the windows at the courthouse."

"The man's a real sweetheart," Betty agreed. "Of course, that only works if you're a doctor donating time out of the goodness of your heart. Those of us on staff are considered slave labor. Last year I agreed to pull the weeds out of Judge Baker's rose garden. Gallagher neglected to tell me that the judge had set aside five acres for those damned prickly things." She extended her hands. "Want to see the scars?"

Forrest Gallagher's baritone voice resounded throughout the room, but his eyes were on Betty Lou as he began his speech. "Before the veterans of this auction dissuade the newcomers from volunteering to the full extent of their generosity, I will remind you all that within a few months construction begins on our new wing. I'm sure all of you know how important it is that we on staff show our complete and enthusiastic support for this project."

Betty Lou nodded vigorously, attempting to escape from the sharp scrutiny of a pair of brown eyes. Gallagher bestowed a significant smile on her. "I'd better crawl under the table until his speech is over," she whispered behind her hand.

"Good idea," Jeff affirmed under his breath. "Otherwise it's another stint at hard labor for you, my girl."

Gallagher called for his assistant, who would be writing down everyone's donation for the brochure. "Let's get started. I'm most anxious to hear what y'all have decided to donate this year. And remember, any of you who can't think of something you'd like to do, I have several suggestions left open from last year."

Betty Lou's hand went up first. Warning Gallagher not to auction her off to the owner of a mansion, she donated one day's service as a housekeeper. Roxie volunteered to act as a maid for a dinner party. Thinking that sounded easy enough, Jeff quickly volunteered to be a butler.

After twenty minutes, almost everyone in the room had offered some service, ranging from the practical to the ridiculous. Labeled "magic fingers," Beth was talked into donating one of her terrific massages to be given in the privacy of the winning bidder's home. As promised by Gallagher, those unlucky few who couldn't think of something to do were assigned tasks that had been extremely popular the year before.

Window washing and flower bed weeding were two of the least strenuous services put to them. Looking like convicts on a chain gang, they left the room grumbling and vowing to use more forethought in the upcoming year. Having gained one hundred percent participation from his employees, the center's administrator walked out beaming.

"He's done it again, ladies," Jeff pronounced as soon as Gallagher was out of hearing range. "I've always suspected he's a descendent of the Pied Piper."

"Me, too," Roxie said, laughing as she got up from the table. "And it's time this rat slinks back to her burrow, where all her little rats are waiting to be fed."

Betty Lou followed her out, saying her husband and two kids were expecting her to join them for a feast at McDonald's. That left Jeff and Beth, who decided to eat supper together. Beth called for a pizza and Jeff agreed to pick it up on his way to her apartment.

Beth was between mouthfuls of pepperoni and cheese, when Jeff reminded her of something she hadn't thought of beforehand. As one of the Shelton Center's private benefactors, a representative of the Towers Foundation would be attending the auction. What if it was Brian?

THAT QUESTION was still on Beth's mind the night of the auction. Adjusting her skirt over her crossed legs, she tried to appear relaxed. She was seated with the rest of the staff on the raised dais at the front of the ballroom. Achieving anything close to a nonchalant air while in the limelight was next to impossible. She, as were her colleagues and a scattering of more notable local personalities, was on display for the bidders' perusal, along with the tangible items arrayed on the long tables that flanked the dais.

Columbus's merchants, as well as its eminent and not-so eminent citizens, had been gracious in their donations to help raise money for the new wing. Original paintings, jewelry, clothing and autographed memorabilia were only a few of the categories the prizes fell into. However, as valuable as most of those items were, the service hours donated by the assembled members of the Shelton Convalescent Center and the celebrities were arousing far more interest.

So far, Roxie's maid service, a personally guided tour of the zoo by its charismatic director and the opportunity to direct the symphony through one number at the next concert had enlivened the bidding and the spirits of the crowd. Serving as auctioneer, Forrest Gallagher was having a field day with this part of the proceedings.

Gradually the atmosphere was taking on the quality of a celebrity roast. It was all being done in good fun and for a good cause, but as Gallagher became more and more effusive in his enticements to the bidders, those waiting on the dais for their turn on the auction block were beginning to cringe.

"The next item on the docket is offered by our handsome, dashing, bachelor doctor, Jeff Samuels," enticed Forrest Gallagher. "He's agreed to be your butler. The bidding will start at one hundred dollars. Who'll give me a hundred?"

An elderly woman at one of the front tables nodded. Gallagher acknowledged the bid and started his rhythmic chant to raise it. After several minutes with the bid rising only by ten-dollar increments, Beth nudged Jeff and teased, "Dr. Dashing, you'd better lend our chief a hand and see if a smile from you can hike that bid up. A hundred dollars won't even pay the rental on your tux."

Jeff arched one of his dark brows at her. "Dr. Dashing? Gallagher's going to have a field day with you, Magic Fingers."

Roxie leaned forward from the second row. "I'd be more concerned about the fingers of whoever wins you as their butler. I know what I'd do with you."

"Hey, Rox, just name the time," Jeff quipped lecherously.

The burst of laughter that followed caused Gallagher to pause in the bidding. "Come on up here, Samuels. Why don't you flash those pearly whites up here where somebody can see them?"

Knowing he had no choice, Jeff prepared to join Gallagher at the podium. With a leering grin, he leaned toward Beth and teased, "No wonder my services aren't going for much. Everybody's holding out for a chance to have your pretty hands on them. Might want to throw in a bid of my own."

With a pointed glare, Beth shooed Jeff toward Gallagher. "Get up there *ex-friend*."

Beth felt vindicated when, as soon as Jeff arrived at his side, Gallagher prompted him to display his penchant for servitude. A towel appeared from nowhere and was quickly draped over Jeff's arm. He was forced to bow and announce that dinner was served.

A few chuckles came from the crowd, but no one raised the bid. Part of the entertainment of the evening was the cajoling and oftentimes hilarious methods Gallagher used to entice high bidding. Everyone, including Gallagher, would have been disappointed if the process had gone quickly and smoothly.

In a whispered aside to Beth, Roxie offered, "If Jeff stripped off that stiff formal shirt and flexed a few muscles, things would get really interesting."

"Roxie Valentine! This is a charity auction, not a night at Chippendale's."

Snapping her fingers, Roxie shrugged. "Shucks! I was hoping tonight was my chance to take a gander at our sexy neurologist's bod."

"Roxie!" Beth admonished again. "Isn't that hunk of a husband of yours enough for you?"

Grinning merrily, Roxie returned, "Sure, but I'm not dead. No harm in looking. Tell me, what's Jeff like beneath that tuxedo?"

"How would I know?"

"Aw, come on, Beth. You've gone out with him. Those eyes, that voice, that set of shoulders. I've heard from a nurse or two at Riverside that he's pretty hot stuff."

"That's not the kind of relationship we have," Beth stated firmly. "I've told you before, we're just friends."

"Sold to Mrs. Brian Hadsworth for five hundred dollars! Come on up and sign your claim."

Gallagher's triumphant announcement sent Beth's pulse racing. It was several seconds before she realized it hadn't been Brian Towers's name that had been announced. Ever since Jeff had reminded her that some member of the Towers family would be in attendance at tonight's affair, she'd been on edge. Uncomfortable about seeing them again, she'd hoped for a last-minute attack of the flu as an excuse to stay home. Unfortunately one could never seem to find a cooperative virus when one needed it.

Resigned to the possibility of seeing Brian, she'd dressed very carefully for the evening. Pure, feminine vanity had prompted her to blow a large portion of her paycheck on a new outfit. The pale peach silk dress featured in the window of a boutique had caught her eye, and within minutes she'd found herself back outside the store with a box containing the dress, appropriate accessories and the skimpiest, most scandalous set of matching lingerie she'd ever owned.

The dress was an elegant design that took advantage of the draping qualities of the fabric. Sari-style, it fell from one shoulder and left the other bare. The small, flat bow that held it in place gave the impression that one tug and the silk would fall in a pool at her feet. To add to the exotic flavor of the dress, she had a serpentine gold bracelet on her upper arm and had brushed her hair all to one side, where it lay in a golden-brown coil on her bare shoulder.

While Jeff was still occupied making arrangements with the winning bidder for his services, Beth scanned the crowd for any sign of Brian. Her exterior might have conveyed a coolly composed sophisticate, but inside she was a mass of nerves. What was she going to say if she ran into Brian? How would he react to seeing her again?

"You're up next," Jeff said, bringing Beth back to the present. "This is the moment everyone's been waiting for."

Beth sent him a quelling glare that had no effect on the brightness of his grin. She had no time to add further admonishment as Gallagher asked her to come to the podium and be introduced.

"The lovely Beth Crosby, therapist *extraordinaire*, has graciously agreed to give a professional massage in the privacy of the winning bidder's home," Gallagher announced. "This is your chance to experience the magic and talented fingers of an expert, my friends. Who wishes to step into her parlor?"

If Forrest Gallagher weren't the administrative head of the Shelton Center, Beth would have gladly kicked him in the shins for that question. Though the crowd was composed of Columbus's wealthiest and most aristocratic people, she still cringed inwardly as she waited for some suggestive remark.

None came and Beth realized that she probably had the sudden presence of Clarissa Gallagher beside her husband to thank for the rescue. Quiet-spoken and gracious, Clarissa was the epitome of Southern femininity and class. Nobody ever stepped the slightest inch beyond the boundaries of good taste when Clarissa was present. It was she who gave the opening remarks that started the bidding.

"Ladies, a soothing massage is just the thing to relax y'all after a hard day in your office, pushin' an ol' heavy sweeper around the house, or after an afternoon runnin' after a ball on the tennis court or golf links. Now who'll start the biddin'?"

The first offer was a flattering two hundred dollars from a silver-haired matron dripping in designer silk and jewels. After such a high start, Beth expected the raises to be small, but they jumped along at a fifty-dollar click. The bidding was lively and good-natured, coming from both women and men.

Forrest Gallagher was in his glory, chanting the bids and urging them ever higher like a professional auctioneer. "I've got five, who'll give me six, six, give me six? I've got six and a half, who'll give me seven?"

"One thousand," a deep male voice drawled from the back of the ballroom.

Gallagher hesitated for a second or two, then chanted the bid and asked for more. The bid rose to two, then five thousand dollars by the same unseen man at the back. From Beth's place at the dais, she couldn't see the bidder, but she knew who it was.

The bid rose rapidly, with Brian continually upping it to the next thousand, until only one other man besides himself remained. People leaned back in their chairs, turning expectantly to see just how high the persistent bidder intended to go. A tall man with blond hair and wide, square shoulders leaned against the archway that separated the ballroom from the lounge.

Beth stared. He looked like Brian, sounded like Brian, but his manner, some indefinable air about him, didn't fit the image of the Brian she knew.

He was dressed in formal evening clothes, as were all the men at the function. Unlike some, who wore the stiffly starched shirts and elegantly tailored jackets uncomfortably, he seemed to carry the ensemble as naturally as he did sweatsuits. The midnight fabric that hugged his shoulders contrasted sharply with his fair coloring, emphasizing the piercing blue of his eyes— eyes that were directed solely at Beth. His gaze cut across the yards that separated them and he blinked twice. *Yes.*

Beth felt the pull on all her senses and everyone else in the room faded away. She wasn't conscious of sound, of anyone, or anything, save the strikingly handsome man staring at her from the back of the room. He was achingly familiar, yet a stranger. It was only a brief moment in actual time, but it seemed far longer as silent messages sailed between them.

Brian was telling her something, but before Beth was able to interpret, his eyes shuttered and she was closed out. Sounds, colors, scents returned and they were no longer alone, nor did they share silent, unique communication.

Gallagher had resumed his chanting until, as if tired of his own game, Brian raised both his hands with his fingers outspread. "Ten thousand!"

At first a shocked silence pervaded the audience, then the gavel sounded and there was a thunderous round of applause. While Beth stepped toward the claims desk to make arrangements for the massage, Brian slowly made his way through the crowd.

8

STUNNED BY BRIAN'S BID, Beth forgot about her trepidation over seeing him again and the obligation she would soon have to him. When he joined her at the claim's table to fill out his check, she wasn't thinking about having to give him a massage; her mind was still reeling at the amount he'd paid for the privilege. Ten thousand dollars! He had magnanimously paid ten thousand dollars for an hour of her time! "I don't know what to say, Brian," she began, intending to thank him for his generosity, but she was cut off before she could finish.

"How about hello? Or nice to see you again?" Brian suggested as he straightened from the table and turned to face her.

Beth felt the impact from her head to her toes. Tall and lean, resplendent in his dark evening clothes, he appeared the epitome of masculine power and vitality. His blond hair gleamed like gold, drawing her appreciative eyes. But it was the slightly arrogant, completely self-confident expression he wore that really threw her. Even his eyes glittered with assurance.

Beth could see nothing to suggest that he'd once been completely paralyzed, that he'd lost five years out of his life or that he'd spent the past year playing catch-up. "Of course it's nice seeing you again." Beth struggled to get the words out. "I was talking about...what I meant was..."

She started and stopped, then blurted, "Brian, you look fantastic!" She expected the grin that followed her impulsive comment, but not the worldly force that came with it. Gone was the vulnerability, the endearing boyish quality of his smiles, and in its place was mocking male amusement. She was completely disconcerted by what he did next.

He let his gaze fall to her smooth tanned shoulders and down the bodice of her exotic dress to her long, shapely legs, encased in pastel peach stockings. His eyes moved back up slowly, past her slender neck and over the delicate planes of her face to her soft mouth. As her lips parted on a startled gasp, he drawled, "You look pretty fantastic yourself, Beth. More beautiful than I remembered."

If Beth thought she was going to have trouble finding words to thank him for his charitable donation, it was nothing compared to the difficulty she had responding to his low, husky compliment. When he lowered his head to bestow a kiss on her cheek, she felt dizzy, and when his warm fingers closed around her elbow, she almost fainted.

"Are you all right?" His voice was all concern as he felt her sway, and his grasp tightened on her arm.

"I...I'm fine," she lied, trying desperately to assimilate all the garbled messages coming and going in her brain. Brian was an old friend, an ex-patient who had his own life now, apart from hers. She should be friendly and polite to him, nothing more.

He was her lover—her heart—come to claim her again. She should throw herself into his arms and never let him go.

She should run while she still had the chance.

"I'll look at my schedule and let you know when to come for that massage," he advised coolly, or warned, or just said. Beth didn't know which.

"That's fine. Let me know." She heard herself agree, but still couldn't believe this was happening. Sometime soon, upon his whim, her hands would be given free license to run all over his body. Her mind boggled at the thought.

She would have to maintain her professional cool, keep her lascivious thoughts to herself. She couldn't wait to get her hands on him, touch him, caress him. She wouldn't do it. She couldn't do it.

Tell him, her brain ordered. *Tell him now.*

"You've gone awfully pale," Brian stated, sliding his arm around her waist. "Has the shock been too much for you?"

"The shock?" Trembling, Beth gazed up into his eyes, and the teasing lights that glimmered there restored her equilibrium. She couldn't let him see what his nearness and touch were doing to her. She gave a light laugh and stepped out of his grasp. "Maybe so. None of my massages have garnered ten thousand dollars before. Forrest Gallagher was thrilled. You were extremely generous, Brian."

For a split second, she thought she saw annoyance in his eyes, but it disappeared with his answer. "The Towers Foundation, not me. We support many events like this one and we always try to give about the same at each."

"I see," Beth replied in a small voice, unaware that her tone conveyed a noticeable pique. Naively she had assumed his high bid had been motivated by personal feeling, not to maintain equitable contributions between the various institutions supported by his wealthy family. Evidently a ten-thousand-dollar donation was nothing out of the ordinary for the Towers Foundation—a mere drop in the bucket.

"That's not to say that one of your massages isn't worth a fortune." Brian's lips twitched at her slighted expression. "Of all people, I should know what those great little hands of yours can do."

For the life of her, Beth couldn't stop the blush that stained her cheeks; it burned even hotter when he chuckled. "I was referring to my therapy sessions, Beth."

She couldn't tell whether he was sincere or not, but she doubted it. This new, much more self-contained Brian would have no trouble dealing with their past intimacy. Unlike her, he might even enjoy reminiscing on the subject. That was to be avoided at all cost. "Well, all of us at the center appreciate your donation very much. We need that new wing."

"Glad to help," Brian tossed back easily. His hand returned to her arm and he began guiding her through the crowd. "Sounds like the last item has come up for bid."

"And Forrest looks like he's just discovered the pot of gold at the end of the rainbow."

"He should," Brian said. "My dad sits on the board, so I know how much was needed to get construction started. Gallagher's gone over the top tonight."

"I didn't know Hadley sat on the board."

"Uh-huh." Brian shrugged, quickening his step when he saw a follow-up question forming on her lips. "You're staying for the dancing, aren't you?"

"I'm sure we are," Beth said, suddenly aware that she'd forgotten all about her escort. She noted Jeff's vacant seat behind the podium. "I wonder where he went."

"Who?"

"Jeff Samuels."

"You came together?"

The question sounded sharp to Beth's ears and she glanced up, but Brian's expression was bland. "Yes." She pointed to the far side of the room. "He's probably waiting for me at our table."

Upon that announcement, Brian hustled her across the room as if she'd suddenly become excess baggage that he couldn't wait to dump. Jeff was in his seat and rose to greet them when they reached the table. Beth saw the question in his eyes as he grabbed hold of

Brian's outstretched hand, but she was spared having to make an answer. Brian did that for her.

"I just dropped by to say hello, Doc," he stated politely. "It's great seeing old friends again." He nodded to include Beth. "Sorry I can't stay and talk, but I'd better get back to my table. Melinda must be wondering what happened to me."

"I read in the paper that you two were an item," Jeff said as he pulled out Beth's chair and she sat down. "Not a bad catch, Towers. She's a great-looking lady."

"I'll tell her you said so," Brian replied. He lifted his hand in a short wave and turned away from the table.

"Why don't you tell her to remind you that you're two months overdue on a physical." Jeff's words brought Brian back around. "Maybe you'll keep your next appointment if she gives you a nudge. Next Friday at three?"

An odd gleam shone in Brian's eyes, but his voice couldn't have been more pleasant. "I'm sure you remember Ben Morley. He's been our family physician for years. Since I no longer need to be under the care of a neurologist, I've gone back to him. I thought my office told you that when they called to cancel."

"No, but I'm always the last to know what goes on in my practice," Jeff replied with commendable aplomb. "I'll make sure Ben gets your records. He's a fine physician. You've placed yourself in good hands."

Brian nodded. "Glad you think so." A few seconds of uncomfortable silence went by, then he made his second farewell. "Maybe I'll see you two on the dance floor later on."

"Sure," Jeff agreed, and sat down, watching Brian until he disappeared in the crowd at the opposite side of the huge ballroom. "Can't say I'm surprised."

"Surprised at what?" Beth asked, reaching for the nearest wineglass and tossing down several swallows in unladylike haste.

"That I've been replaced as Brian's physician. I was never his favorite person."

"He liked you," Beth assured him. "I think he just doesn't want any reminders of a time he'd much rather forget. It's off with the old and on with the new." Her voice faltered on the adage, tears smarting behind her eyes. She was the old, and beautiful, talented Melinda Graham was the new.

"Perhaps," Jeff agreed thoughtfully. "I also know he was so jealous of me he wanted to smash my face if I so much as looked at you."

"Oh, come on, Jeff. Why would you think that?"

"Hey, I've got brains as well as beauty."

Beth laughed, shaking her head as she allowed a waiter to refill her wineglass. "Well, your beauty is safe from him now, unless you start making eyes at Melinda Graham."

"No more sparks between the two of you?"

Beth hesitated a little too long before answering, "I guess not."

"At least not on Brian's part?"

Making a valiant effort not to cry, Beth admitted, "No, not on his part."

"I'm sorry," Jeff said sympathetically. "But you knew this might happen. That's why you left him when you did."

"Yes."

Jeff placed his hand over hers. "As much as it hurts you now, you did the right thing, a really nice thing. Not many women could resist a guy like Brian."

Beth didn't tell him that where Brian was concerned, she had no resistance at all. She may have done the right thing by leaving him, but not before they'd made long, beautiful, unforgettable love. She closed her eyes as the memory washed over her. She thought of the small, delicate wildflower that had seemed to symbolize her fleeting time with Brian. It hadn't survived her return to the house, nor had Brian's love endured the test of time.

"Give it a while," Jeff advised softly. "Somewhere out there is a man who deserves you. If I weren't so fickle, I'd offer myself."

Good friend that he was, Jeff was always able to entice her out of her despondency. Her eyes came open, warm with affection. "You're not fickle. You just need variety."

"A variety of blondes, brunettes and redheads." Jeff toasted her with his glass, gray eyes dancing as they glanced off the peach silk of her bodice.

"Dirty old man!" Beth scoffed.

"Wanna dance with me, honey?" Jeff inquired in his best lecherous tone.

"That depends." She pretended to consider. "Are we going out there so you can get a better look at all the young lovelies gathered up for this occasion?"

"Never." Jeff tried to look offended, and failed miserably. "I always love the one I'm with."

Beth laughed and downed the remaining contents of her wineglass. "How commendable, Doctor. Let's go."

Jeff was an expert dancer. To follow his intricate steps, Beth couldn't concentrate on anything else. The amount of alcohol she'd consumed in so short a time, didn't make the task easy, but soon their partnership on the dance floor became as comfortable as the one they had off it. As Jeff whirled her around the polished parquet floor, she realized they were causing a minisensation with the bystanders. "Striking couple, aren't they?" she heard one comment as Jeff bent her over his arm at the end of a fast tango.

The orchestra barely paused before going into their next number, a slow waltz. "Thank heavens," Beth murmured, resting her head on Jeff's chest. "I'm feeling pretty dizzy."

"I'd like you to meet Melinda Graham," Brian said, tapping Jeff on the shoulder as the sound of violins swelled in romantic harmony. "Melinda and I were watching you two tango. We thought you might like to restore your depleted energy with fresh partners during this slow number."

"Love to." Jeff turned traitor at first sight of the spectacular blonde woman draped in clinging gold lamé who was offering her hand to him. Evidently deciding further introductions were a waste of time, he grasped the elegant fingers and twirled Melinda away before Beth got the chance to open her mouth.

So much for Jeff's love-the-one-you're-with philosophy, she thought miserably as she struggled to get her bearings. Where did that leave her? With Brian—that's where. And Jeff was supposed to be her friend.

"Beth?" Head cocked, Brian was waiting for her to step into his arms. "I may not be as good a dancer as Samuels, but I won't stamp on your feet."

Sensing her reluctance, he added grimly, "I promise. It won't be that bad."

She wasn't thinking about possible damage to her feet but to her heart when she was pulled into Brian's embrace. "Won't it?" she whispered. Unfortunately he heard.

"My coordination has vastly improved since last we met," he assured her tightly, then set out to prove it.

In an instant, Beth found out his coordination was not the only thing that had been strengthened over the past months. He brought her against him for a rapid turn and her breasts were crushed against a set of hard, well-defined pectorals. His hand spread out against her bare back and she felt the tough calluses that had replaced the almost feminine smoothness of his fingers and palm. Her hips cradled a flat, rock-hard stomach and her legs entwined with strongly muscled thighs.

She had left a man who had been as close to physical perfection as one man could get. As impossible as it seemed, Brian had perfected perfection. She felt hot all over, felt his heat searing into her, and she couldn't help herself. She melted against him like warm, flowing honey. Being so close to him was wonderful; it felt so good.

Brian stiffened as her resistance drained away. But, then, it was as if he, too, were engulfed in a tide of swirling emotion. He executed another turn, then another, faster and faster, until the room disappeared in a moving whirl of bright, distorted colors. Beth couldn't break out of his hold or his mesmerizing gaze; she didn't want to try. As they had in a countless number of her dreams, they moved as one.

Dreams. All those erotic dreams Beth couldn't forget. Arms clinging tightly around his neck, she was flying, floating starward in flight. Together with Brian, the universe, a myriad of vast galaxies, was hers. Being back in his arms was heaven, and she wanted to stay there forever.

Forever lasted only until the end of the dance. Beth lifted heavy lids when Brian stopped moving and the sweeping sounds of violins faded away. Unfortunately the starry expression in her eyes hadn't faded as quickly. Brian would have had to be blind not to read what was in them.

"At least some things never change," he said in a rough whisper as he caught her gazing at his lips. "I want you, too."

His eyes flashed as her breasts heaved in response to his tone and her lips parted on a helpless sigh. "Come on," he urged. Grabbing her by the hand, he began weaving his way through the milling crowd. Beth went where he guided her, oblivious to everything but the memory of the hungry expression that had been in his eyes when he'd gazed down at her.

They exited out the side door to the left of the podium. Without looking back to determine whether she was willing—assuming she was—Brian dragged her down a short hall to the last door near the end. It was a janitorial closet, but as he pulled her in behind him, closing the door and shutting out the light, it became a space of velvety shadow.

Beth was glad that she couldn't see, for then she'd have had to acknowledge what she was doing. Without offering even a token protest, she received his lips, assuaging the hunger that had ravaged her for over a year. As his tongue did wild, sensuous things to the recesses of her mouth, his hands smoothed over the bareness of her back, his fingers caressing.

"Brian," she whispered huskily, pleading for something that he was more than willing to give.

He muttered something violent and then splayed one hand over her buttocks, pressing her against the evidence of his arousal. His other hand was at her shoulder, releasing the silken bow and the soft flesh it had concealed. His mouth made her into his obedient slave; she complied with its demands, arching her back and crying out at the feel of his tongue encircling her sensitive nipple.

"Touch me, Beth. Unbutton my shirt and touch me," he whispered against her skin. "Let me feel your mouth on me."

Enclosed in a world of their own, a world of mindless passion and need, Beth could no more have refused him than stopped breathing. Her trembling fingers fluttered to his chest as he straightened, moving slightly away from her. She slipped her hands beneath his jacket, sliding it off his shoulders and down his muscled arms. She tugged his shirt out of his pants and fumbled with the buttons, but his fingers met hers on the third one, opening it before she could manage.

Beneath her questing, curious, excited hands, his chest rose and fell with his increasingly ragged breathing. When her lips touched him he shuddered, arching his spine just as she had done at the feel of his mouth on her. "I have to," he ground out, but she didn't know what he meant until his hands closed on her arms.

He brought her inside his shirt, groaning when he felt her warm, bare skin against his chest. His hands moved to her sides, caressing in slow, upward sweeps that approached her quivering breasts, then retreated. When he heard the tiny cry of frustration she made, he stepped back a little, waiting for his eyes to adjust to the dark.

He lifted his head to look at her; his palms cupped her breasts and his thumbs rubbed with tormenting leisure against the sensitized tips. "The last time I held you like this the sun was shining. I could see every delectable inch of you and watch your reaction to my touch. Open your eyes, Beth. See how beautiful you are in a different kind of light."

Beth's lashes fluttered and her eyes opened, not so much in response to his soft-spoken request as to its evocative tone. Instantly she wished she had kept her eyes closed, for she was given a picture of herself that would be forever burned into her memory. There was a line of small, square windows near the ceiling of the outside wall that they hadn't noticed when they'd first entered the closet. Now, eyes adjusted to the darkness, they could both see what had previously gone unseen. Cupped in Brian's hands, her breasts were bathed in moonlight. As if cast in silver by a sculptor's hand, they glowed in opalescent beauty against a backdrop of dark velvet shadow.

"'How silver-sweet sound lovers' tongues by night,'" Brian quoted from *Romeo and Juliet* as he lifted her breasts more fully in his palms and lowered his head. "And these a priceless gift from the gods."

A piercing shaft of desire went through her as his mouth closed over one breast and his lover's tongue delighted the nipple. As long as she lived she would never forget the wondrous feeling, or the sight of his head, golden hair brushed with silver light, nestled against her bared breasts. He adored her nakedness with his mouth, his hands and eyes, until Beth felt as if she might faint with joy. He pleased her in ways no man had done or ever would do again.

After endless moments of exquisite pleasure, Brian pulled back. He couldn't go on with this. He'd let his desire for her overwhelm him, but this wasn't the time or place to act on it. He didn't know how deeply involved she was with Jeff Samuels. Though the thought of them together filled him with jealousy, he had to find out no matter how painful it was.

His harsh breathing echoed loudly in the silence, but it was nothing compared to the wild pounding of Beth's heart. "Brian?"

"Enough!" he bit out. "If this goes any further, I'll be taking you standing up in a broom closet. You know that, don't you?"

Yes, she knew that, but before he'd spoken, she wouldn't have cared. She was aching for him, blind to sense and to reason. When he switched on the light, she was blinded to all else but the glaring reality of what had almost happened. In a closet filled with mops, pails and cleaning supplies, she'd almost given herself to a man she hadn't seen in over a year, a man she no longer knew.

Frantically she pulled at the silk bunched around her waist. Head down, cheeks flaming, she covered her breasts and retied the bow at her shoulder. "Turn off that light," she pleaded in an agony of embarrassment.

"It's a little late for that," Brian pointed out. "Besides, if we can't see enough to make ourselves presentable, we'll have to stay in here all night." Another surge of jealousy hit him as he thought of her going home with another man. "I doubt Samuels will leave without searching for you. Do you want him to find us looking like we've just—"

"Don't say it!" Beth was mortified by the picture he provoked in her mind. What if Jeff or anyone else had opened the door and seen what they'd been doing? "Don't even think it!" She stared at Brian's bare chest, his nipples still aroused to tiny pinpoints. She was appalled by the telling marks of her lipstick on the bronzed skin. "Button your shirt!"

"Yes, ma'am," Brian said meekly, but took his time following orders, aware that her eyes followed every movement of his hands. "After a year, Jeff Samuels still can't claim your whole heart, can he? If he could, you wouldn't have come in here with me. Admit it."

Beth was stunned by the satisfaction and triumph in his voice. "Admit what?"

"That you still feel something for me that refuses to die. That you want me more than you've ever wanted that playboy doctor." Realizing that she wasn't about to admit any such thing, he asked the question that had been on his mind all night. "Are you sleeping with him?"

In the shocked silence that followed, Brian slipped his black satin tie from under his collar and shoved it into his pocket before stuffing his shirt into his trousers. Bending over to retrieve his jacket from the floor, he brushed off the dust that clung to the black material, put it on, then repeated the question. "Well, are you?"

Except for the missing black tie, Brian looked none the worse for wear. Beth knew she looked as if she'd just been doing exactly what she'd been doing, and that fired her temper almost as much as his presumptuous inquiry concerning her personal life. "That's none of your business!"

"I think it is," he disagreed, his fingers curling possessively around the gleaming tawny coil of her hair and rearranging it on her bare shoulder. "You just made it my business. Or do you duck into closets and bare your breasts to every man you meet?"

"Of course not!" she spluttered.

"I didn't think so." He smiled at her affronted face, but gave up his pursuit of an answer concerning the depth of her involvement with Jeff. "It really doesn't matter if you've gone to bed with Samuels or not. You know what I was telling you during the bidding. After this, he'd better know it, too."

Confusion added to the humiliation and outrage flashing darkly in her eyes. "I don't know what you're talking about. I wasn't aware of you telling me anything during the bidding."

"No?" His eyebrows rose. "Then your nonverbal communication skills must have grown a little rusty from disuse." He blinked twice, signaling yes, but she had no more idea what he was trying to convey this time than she'd had the last.

"Yes, what?"

"Yes, to us," he stated firmly, blue eyes sparkling with challenge as he captured her chin and kissed her. Once certain that she couldn't doubt what he was feeling, he gave her the words. "Here I come Elizabeth Ann Crosby. Ready or not, here I come."

Beth gaped at him in disbelief. Brian chuckled, a low, sexy sound from deep in his throat. "You're ready now, but this isn't the time or the place."

He opened the door a crack and peered outside, then stepped into the hallway. "I'll make sure no one gets in here until you're prepared to face the public."

By the time Beth was prepared for that, he was no longer in sight. When she rejoined Jeff at their table, he told her that Brian and Melinda Graham had left, saying they had to drop in at another party before calling it a night.

Before Beth was able to call it a night herself, it was the next morning. In bed, her exhausted body finally gave in to its need for rest, but her brain refused to shut off, repeating the same words over and over again, "Ready or not, here I come."

9

BETH TURNED her vacuum cleaner off and pushed the elderly, heavy device back over the spotless wall-to-wall carpeting that covered the floors of her efficiency apartment. "Your laundry's done and this place is cleaner than it's been for a month. So what are you going to do with the rest of the day?" she asked aloud as she jostled the cleaner into a position between her tennis racket and an assortment of items that had found their way into her front closet.

A can of tennis balls toppled from a shelf and emptied its contents across the foyer floor. Spending the next hour or so organizing the closet crossed her mind as she captured the last yellow ball. Giving it a test bounce, she doubted it was worth saving. But she popped it into the can and replaced the set on the shelf.

Going through the contents of the closet would be an admirable thing to do, and Lord knew she had nothing better to occupy her time. Nevertheless she carefully pushed the door closed, crossing her fingers that everything would stay in place. A glance at her watch confirmed that most of Saturday still lay before her. It was not even noon. Whatever had possessed her to get up at the crack of dawn and throw herself into a fit of cleaning?

"Because you couldn't lie in bed any longer!" Sleep hadn't been particularly easy during the two weeks since the auction. Actually, sleep hadn't been so difficult; it was the dreams that continually haunted her slumbers that made her so restless.

"'To sleep: perchance to dream: ay, there's the rub,'" Beth quoted. Like Shakespeare's Hamlet, Beth's dreams gave her pause and she suffered the pangs of love deprived as painfully as had that melancholy prince of Denmark. Oh, poor Hamlet certainly had other things besides the loss of his Ophelia weighing heavily upon him, Beth allowed, but who was to say he suffered more from the "whips and scorns of time" than she?

Time! Two weeks of time to be precise. "Ready or not, here I come," Brian had told her. So where was he? Each day she'd waited for a call, a note, some kind of communication. If he wasn't planning to follow through on the personal challenge he'd issued, she'd still expected to hear whether or not he wanted the massage he'd paid for so dearly. She realized that his ten thousand dollars was a charity offering and often patrons didn't claim the service they'd bid on, but she'd been positive Brian would.

At least she had been for the first few days. Now she wasn't so sure. Had Brian substituted that scorching interlude in the closet for the massage? In retrospect, had he felt that he'd already gotten what he'd paid for? It was a humiliating prospect she'd considered and steadfastly rejected. At the end of the second week with no word from him, however, she had to give credence to that theory or others even harder to accept.

Perhaps a certain blonde newscaster had earned the right to demand that no other hands but hers would touch Brian's body. If that was the case, Beth doubted she'd ever hear from him again. She couldn't compete with Melinda Graham on any level and expect to come out on top. Even so, the jealous rage that surged through her whenever she pictured Brian with Melinda shocked her and made her even angrier with herself than she was with him.

More disturbing was the possibility that she and Melinda could be two of many. What if Brian had so many eager women on the string he had difficulty arranging time for them in his busy schedule? Or could it be that he'd viewed that episode in the closet as the wrapping up of some unfinished business, satisfying a challenge left unanswered between them?

Maybe the response she'd given him had soothed his male ego and another demonstration of her vulnerability to him was no longer such an urgent need. If that was true, she didn't know whether to treat his continued silence as a slap in the face or a lucky break.

"What am I supposed to do? Walk around on pins and needles while he decides whether I'm worth the effort it would take to talk me into his bed?" she demanded as she headed toward her bathroom and a much needed shower. "There should have been some kind of time limit on the validity of his claim."

A time limit would have kept her from feeling as if she had to be in a constant state of readiness. As it was, every time her phone rang she expected it to be Brian, and her nerves were constantly on edge. She wasn't sure how much longer she was going to be able to stand the suspense.

"One more week of this and that's it," she declared with finality as she stepped from the shower and reached for a towel.

As if it had been waiting for just such a cue, her doorbell began ringing. Beth froze. *Brian.* Her flesh broke out in goose bumps despite the steamy warmth of the bathroom. With shaking fingers she grabbed a towel and wrapped it around her dripping head. The doorbell's insistent ringing increased her nervousness as she ran into her bedroom.

"It's not Brian. It's not Brian. It's probably the paperboy," she chanted as she wrapped a terry robe around her dripping body and ran through the apartment.

At the door, she paused, took a deep, calming breath, then turned the knob. It wasn't Brian. It wasn't the paperboy, either. A uniformed chauffeur stood in the hallway.

"Miss Crosby?" he asked, not one line of his face betraying any shock at addressing a woman dripping a puddle of water on her foyer floor.

Beth nodded affirmation of her identity.

"I'm here on behalf of Mr. Brian Towers." said the man Beth judged to be about sixty years old. He continued, "I've been instructed to wait as long as it might take you to get ready, but not to return without you."

Beth's face must have registered her shock at the imperious-sounding instruction, for the man quickly added, "Mr. Towers indicated you would be expecting this . . . ah . . ."

"Summons?" Beth supplied tightly, struggling to keep from directing her anger at this man. It wasn't his fault if his employer was commanding her time like some arrogant potentate. "I'm afraid Mr. Towers wasn't specific about the day or time of our appointment."

The chauffeur's formal demeanor slipped and he took off his hat, worrying it restlessly with his hands. "I am sorry, Miss Crosby. I'm afraid there's been some lack of communication. It's obvious that you knew nothing about this.

"It's not like Mr. Towers to let something like this happen," he hastened to add as if he felt driven to further apologize for his employer's actions. "He's been awfully busy lately and I'm sure that's why he didn't call you himself. He probably told one of his secretaries to inform you and somehow the message was lost."

I'll just bet! Beth wanted to shout, but managed to refrain by gritting her teeth. This high-handedness was a perfect example of the difference she'd sensed in Brian upon seeing him again. He might still be considered a junior executive, but she knew not even the heir apparent of a company as big as Towers Enterprises would rise so rapidly without having learned how to wield power ruthlessly. When he wiggled his little finger, he expected people to jump.

In one year, he'd undergone a meteoric rise in the company and would probably step into the presidency very shortly. He couldn't have risen so far so fast without being totally single-minded. Beth didn't know why that surprised her. Within moments of his recovery, he'd been raring to go, pushing himself to the limit of his endurance.

Despite her rising ire at Brian's lack of courtesy, Beth felt sorry for the chauffeur's obvious discomfort with the situation. Now that the man had lost most of his formal facade, she sensed a gentle, almost grandfatherly spirit within him. She guessed that his blue eyes could sparkle with warmth and laughter and that his mouth was more comfortable with kindly smiles than stiff reserve.

She stepped away from the door and indicated that he should come inside. "It's not your fault—"

"Edmund," he supplied.

"Uh, Edmund. Brian...er...Mr. Towers has made the mistake, not you," she said calmly, though inside she was raging. Brian Hadley Towers III certainly had made a mistake and he was going to hear about it. Though it was tempting to send Edmund back to his employer with a curt message, Beth decided to deliver it in person. Edmund would never be able to tell Brian that she was not some concubine in a harem that he could summon at will.

"Why don't you make yourself comfortable while I get dressed," she invited, directing Edmund toward her living room. "Mr. Towers may have to wait awhile."

As regally as anyone dressed in a flowered terry turban and a rather worn bathrobe could, Beth left the chauffeur and glided toward her bedroom. Once the door was closed behind her, she moved into a flurry of preparations. The towel and robe went flying as she rummaged through her drawer for underwear, her mind racing as she contemplated how she should dress for this occasion.

She was still undecided when she stood staring into her closet. It wasn't until she spied a white uniform hanging at the back that she made her choice. After she delivered a thorough setdown for his presumptive manner, Brian was going to get a very impersonal, highly professional massage by a woman who'd flunk out of any harem.

"How dare he think all I've done for two weeks is sit around and wait for him to call me," she raged under her breath as she pulled on the white knit slacks and zipped up the matching top. She plopped down on the corner of her bed and tied the laces to the gum-soled nursing shoes that went with the uniform.

So what if she had been waiting around? He'd never know it. What gall to presume she had nothing else to do on her day off. What conceit to think she didn't have any plans. Even if she didn't, she certainly did now.

She was going to pummel his body until he screamed for mercy. He'd be so bruised from her ministrations he

wouldn't be waggling any fingers at anybody for quite
some time. She'd rub so much camphorated oil into his
muscles he'd stink for a week. With any luck, Melinda
Graham's eyes would water if she got anywhere near
him.

Coiling her still wet hair into a tight bun at her nape,
she relished the thought of the agony she was going to
inflict on him. She flexed her supposedly magic fingers. *Black magic.* She chortled evilly.

As she sat in the luxurious back seat of the long, sleek
Lincoln, Beth prepared her opening speech. The night
of the auction she had fallen into his arms like a ripe
peach, but if he touched her again Brian would bite into
the pit. She'd been crazy to spend all this time hoping
they might get back together someday. From all indications, the man she had fallen in love with no longer
existed.

She must have been crazy. She was still crazy, Beth
thought the instant Brian opened the door of his apartment. He looked even better than he'd looked at the
auction. A baby-blue cashmere sweater that matched
the heavenly color of his eyes covered his broad shoulders and chest. Faded jeans hung low on his lean hips
and hugged his long legs.

He was smiling a slow, sexy smile that turned her
brain to mush. She mumbled some inane response to
his greeting and forgot every word of the scathing put
down she'd rehearsed during the drive across town.

"Thanks for coming, Beth, you can't know how
badly I need you," he said, ushering her inside, his voice

and words wrapping around her as warmly as his smile. "I'm sure glad my secretary was able to arrange this with you."

His statement confirmed Edmund's assertion that there had been a breakdown in communications. Beth felt some of her anger dissipating. He looked so tired. It would be cruel to tear into him for something that might not have been his fault, after all.

His smile was the lopsided, endearing one she remembered. Her resolve to be coldly removed from him was melting, replaced by a different restraint. Brian's body seemed stiff. His movements disjointed and slow, either due to exhaustion or unease, she couldn't be sure. The openness of his nature and the transparency of his feelings, once so easy to read, were now shielded behind a self-contained mask. Whether in empathetic response to the tension she sensed in him or because of the spread of unsureness that pervaded her, Beth felt her own body grow tense.

His voice was husky, tinged with fatigue and something else. Desire? Real need for her?

His next statement erased her wishful thinking. "I've been looking forward to this since I boarded the plane in Melbourne yesterday. Or was it the day before?" He pushed a hand through his hair, then wiped his palm down over his face. Shaking his head as if to clear it, he admitted. "I've lost all track of time. It is Saturday here, isn't it?"

"Yes," Beth answered, frowning at the gray pallor that dulled his bronzed skin. She couldn't hide her concern as she asked, "How long were you in Australia?"

"I left right after that shindig for the Shelton Center," he supplied as he slipped her tote bag from her shoulder. "In two weeks I've seen the inside of enough grocery stores to last me a lifetime. I stopped counting after the first twenty."

"Tight schedule," Beth replied, masking her elation with a sympathetic smile. Brian hadn't been with Melinda Graham or any other woman during the past two weeks, unless he'd managed to find one in an Australian grocery store. From his description of his itinerary, she didn't think that he had.

Grasping the strap of her bag in one hand, he casually placed his other at the small of her back and guided her toward his living room. "I appreciate your coming."

In the middle of the room, Brian dropped his hand from her back. Beth took another step or two before she realized he was no longer following her. She'd assumed he was going to guide her straight to wherever he wanted the massage to take place. Looking about the room, she didn't see anywhere appropriate other than the lushly carpeted floor.

Turning toward him, she was about to question him, when he asked, "What do you think of the place?"

The query took her off guard, especially as it was accompanied by an expression of hopeful expectancy. She gave the room another sweeping glance. There was no mistaking that everything in it was brand-new and

expensive. What she saw reflected the tastes of a man
who'd come a long way from the boy who'd occupied
that cozy bedroom at the Towerses' mansion.

The contemporary decor of the penthouse apartment atop the Towers Building was in sharp contrast
with the warm antiques that graced the country estate.
Here in the living room, two walls were solid smoked
glass with no draperies to soften the stark lines.
Chrome, glass and leather furnishings mixed with the
softer pieces upholstered in a dove-gray suede. The gray
was carried through in the carpeting of an identical
shade and echoed in the lighter walls. The only color
in the room was in the bright oils and prints scattered
artfully across the walls. Yet somehow everything
pulled together to create an inviting atmosphere.

"It's very nice, Brian. Very sophisticated, very appropriate for a rising executive and one of Columbus's
most eligible bachelors," she confirmed.

Her answer seemed to please him, for he sent her another of his smiles that so reminded her of days past,
and thereby eroded her defenses. "Thanks, I hoped
you'd like it. This space has been sitting up here unused for years. My grandfather had it built, but World
War II intervened and the penthouse never got completed. It took a few months to renovate it and make it
habitable."

Unable to stop herself, Beth moved toward the windows. All of Columbus seemed to be lying at her feet,
or perhaps it was lying at the feet of the man who presently occupied the penthouse.

The state office buildings glimmered white in the sunshine, looking like sugar brick models from this far up. The Scioto River, a silver ribbon, threaded its way along the edge of the main business district of the city. The grass along the river's edge was like a green velvet trim, embroidered here and there by trees taking on the first colors of approaching autumn.

"What a beautiful view," Beth complimented him breathlessly. "What a terrible waste that this apartment has gone unused all these years."

The lyrics of an old song drifted into Beth's mind. *"On a clear day, you can see forever"*. The day was clear. Puffs of clouds dotted a bright-blue sky. She could almost imagine that she could see the green and gold fields that lay beyond the city. Peering to the north, she could see the tops of the two towering dormitories Ohio State University students lovingly referred to as the "silos."

Beyond these loomed the massive gray coliseum, where the scarlet-and-gray clad warriors of the university defended their honor. It had been within that cement horseshoe-shaped stadium that Brian had experienced moments of glory and one horrible moment of tragic defeat. She wondered what he thought when he viewed the stadium. Had he attended any of the games last fall? He'd watched football on television during his convalescence, but would it be so easy to walk into that very stadium where he'd been injured?

Brian tossed Beth's tote bag onto one of the couches that defined a conversation area. That view wasn't all

that had been wasted, he thought, studying the uni-
form-clad woman standing by the windows. He smiled
at the reasoning she'd probably used in choosing the
crisp, white attire. It screamed "I'm a professional.
Don't get any other ideas, buster."

He'd expected something like this, and had almost
laughed when he'd opened the door a few minutes ago
and seen her. Obviously Beth had forgotten that he was
a sucker for a woman in uniform. He wondered how
much else she'd forgotten. He'd forgotten nothing,
especially not the wisdom she'd offered before telling
him goodbye.

Taking her advice, he'd tackled a lot in the past year
and succeeded in accomplishing each of his goals. Only
one challenge remained, and she was finally here on his
turf. In three strides, he could be across the room and
have her in his arms. She would capitulate as easily as
she had two weeks ago, but he wanted so much more
than her body.

Curling his palms into fists, he held them stiffly at his
sides and kept his feet firmly planted in the middle of
the room. Patience, he reminded himself. The penthouse hadn't been completed in a day, nor would Beth's
compliance to live in it with him be accomplished that
quickly.

"I'll give you a quick tour of the place and then we'll
have lunch," he said, breaking into Beth's contempla-
tion of the view.

"Lunch?" Beth turned away from the window, a
frown furrowing her brows. "I didn't come here for

lunch, Brian. I came to give you a massage. I donated an hour of my time and I'm afraid that's all I can give you."

Brian shifted his weight and propped his hand on one lean hip. He tilted his head to the side, surveyed her and sent her another of his special grins. "Okay, so you're a busy woman. An hour it is. However, I happen to be starving and I'm going to eat lunch. If we don't get to the massage in an hour, then consider the deal met, anyway."

"I guess I can spare more than an hour," she admitted, knowing she would live to regret it. "We'll have lunch, then you'll have your massage."

"Thanks," Brian said, beaming his pleasure. "After a thirty-six hour flight, every muscle in my body is tighter than a drum."

If she'd still harbored any doubts that this appointment was to be anything but professional, they fled. One look at the man confirmed his assertion that he was a mass of tight muscles. He needed her expertise as a therapist-masseuse. Seduction was the farthest thing from his mind. She didn't know how she felt about that. Relief? Frustration? Hurt.

Brian gave a nod toward the archway at one end of the living room and Beth assumed it led to the dining room. Hoping to lighten the tension that had stretched out between them, she said conversationally, "After so many hours in the air, I know how your body must be feeling."

The minute the statement was out, Beth wanted to swallow it back, unheard, down her throat. She certainly did know what his body felt like. She'd once had months of familiarity with it beneath the ministration of her skilled hands, and then one glorious afternoon when she'd touched every inch of him with the fingertips of a lover. She'd never know a man's body better than she knew Brian's.

She chanced a quick glance to see if he was going to pick up on the remark. She wished she hadn't looked. His lips were pressed tightly together and a mischievous light twinkled in his eyes. It was all too obvious to Beth that he was struggling to keep from making a heated rejoinder. Feigning ignorance of his struggle, she turned her attention toward the dining room and the table set for two.

The small round table was draped to the floor with a crisp gray linen cloth, double layered with a shorter white one. A small arrangement of pink roses sat in the middle and a bottle of champagne was chilling in a stand nearby. Thinking they would be making themselves a sandwich, Beth was overwhelmed by the elegant repast set before her.

Next to the table was a wheeled butler's table heavily laden with food. A linen-draped silver basket held an assortment of rolls. A platter of chilled seafood was nestled in a bed of ice. A crystal bowl of crisp salad greens was surrounded by smaller bowls of dressings, croutons, fruit—all the fixings any salad bar would

boast. A warming tray held several silver-covered dishes.

Raising a skeptical brow, she asked, "This is our lunch?"

He had the good grace to appear at least slightly embarrassed. "Uh . . . it's a way of thanking you for your donation to the center and a welcome back celebration."

Welcome back for whom? she wanted to ask, but feared the answer wouldn't be the one she wanted to hear. Having him welcome her back into his life was too much like a fairy-tale ending to the fairy-tale beginning of their relationship. She no longer believed in fairy tales.

Brian pulled out one of the chairs, and as soon as she was seated he took his own. As if to prove his assertion that he was starving, Brian immediately started filling their plates from the dishes on the server. The food looked and smelled delicious, but she doubted she'd be able to do justice to the mountain Brian placed before her.

He reached for the bottle of champagne and deftly popped the cork without losing a drop. Just as smoothly, he filled both their glasses and raised his in a toast. "To the past and all you did for me," he said as he tapped his glass to hers. "You do have magic—" He paused and smiled broadly. Beth caught her breath, fearing how he might finish the sentence. "Fingers," he finished, and Beth almost let out her pent-up breath in relief. "If I weren't so tired right this minute, I'd flex my biceps to prove how well they work, thanks to you."

Instantly Beth recalled how his body had felt underneath her fingertips when they'd caressed him in that dark closet. She didn't need any more proof. Besides, every time he moved the clingy cashmere of his sweater emphasized his tempting attributes. "I only kept your muscles from atrophying," she said, keeping her attention on his face, which was a temptation in itself. "Any therapist could have done that."

"No, Beth," Brian quickly negated. "You believed and you kept me and everyone else believing, especially Mom."

"Brian, your mother never stopped believing you'd recover. She's the strongest, most positive woman I've ever known."

"She's that all right," he agreed. "However, she's admitted recently that she had her low times and you helped her through them."

Beth gave a slight shrug, reluctantly accepting his praise and his estimation of her abilities. "How are your parents, Brian?"

Brian launched into a lively description of all the activities his parents had thrown themselves into "now that they're no longer tied down to an invalid son." His label for himself was in no way self-pitying. Somehow he was able to make light of that time.

As he talked, Beth surprised herself by being able to put a sizable dent in the food on her plate. Brian couldn't have been a more charming host. Gregarious and gracious, even in his exhaustion, he managed to erase some of Beth's unease by treating her like an old, valued friend. Throughout the conversation, Beth was continually reminded of the differences a year had made in him. He'd filled out magnificently and she doubted she was doing a very good job of masking her purely feminine appreciation of his physique.

He'd packed so much into one short year. The accomplishments were staggering. He'd also matured dramatically. They were almost exactly the same age. Once she'd felt far older than him, but now she felt just the reverse. Somehow, in the span of a year, he'd taken on an urbanity and sophistication she doubted she'd ever match. All her instincts warned her that she could be over her depth if she wasn't very careful.

Even though soft music played from some hidden sound system, the apartment was too quiet. Edmund had directed her to the elevator, then left her. There was no sign of any other members of Brian's personal staff, and Beth was positive they were absolutely alone. Looking down at the sexless uniform she'd worn, she wasn't sure whether she was glad or sorry she'd chosen it.

The white polyester pantsuit was totally out of place in these surroundings. Though the sun was shining brightly into the room, the luncheon was as intimate and seductive as if they'd been dining by candlelight. Across from her sat one of the most attractive men she'd ever known, and she was dressed for work.

The hand resting in her lap clutched the napkin spread across her thighs. Her fingertips were already quivering at the thought of running her hands all over his sleek body. *Pummel* and *pound* were no longer the words to describe what she wanted to do to him. *Fondle* and *caress* were more like it.

"You haven't brought any of your torture devices in that bag, have you?" Brian asked in a sudden change of subject.

"What?"

Brian grinned at her startled expression. "I was just remembering some of your methods of massage," he told her. "I half expected you to show up with Jake in tow, rolling that huge ball you used to stretch me out on."

His teasing tone relaxed her once more and Beth smiled. "Nothing so drastic," she assured him. "Of course, if you'd like, I imagine I could arrange to have that ball delivered, and maybe Edmund could be called in to help."

"Oh, please," Brian begged, throwing up his hands as if to ward off an attack. "Six months of your sadistic methods is enough for any man."

"You should have thought of that before you raised that bid so high no one would top you," she reminded him.

Pushing his chair away from the table, Brian rolled his shoulders. "If you can take out these knots, it'll be the best money I every spent." He drained his champagne glass and looked questioningly toward her. "Are you ready?"

Looking at his drooping eyelids and slumping shoulders, Beth suggested guilelessly, "Wouldn't you rather go to bed?"

Brian's head shot up and his eyes took on a smoldering look as he gazed across the table at her before standing up. Backing away, he muttered thickly, "I wouldn't touch that line with a ten-foot pole."

10

"'ME THINKS THE LADY doth protest too much,'" Brian quoted to himself while Beth babbled on about her concern for his state of exhaustion. As he guided her toward his bedroom, her high color told him that even if her comment about going to bed had been innocent, her thoughts were not. He was very glad of that, even if for the moment he couldn't do anything about it.

With the exception of this one damnably frustrating hitch that he'd steadfastly denied would happen, he'd planned today's meeting down to the last detail. They would talk until Beth felt completely comfortable with him. They would share a delicious lunch, a few glasses of champagne to settle her nerves, then sometime during his massage he would pull her into his arms and do everything he'd dreamed about doing for the past six months.

Unfortunately his body had decided to renege halfway through his second glass of champagne. Either that, or he'd been incapacitated by the worst case of jet lag known to man. Whatever, unless he got some rest he had absolutely no chance of impressing her with his fantastic skills as a lover.

As much as he wanted her, he couldn't take her. At least, not for another few hours. When he made love to Beth Crosby again, he was going to be in top form, and right now he felt like a zombie, his limbs dead weights. A nap. All he needed was a short nap, then everything could continue according to plan.

As soon as they reached the bedroom, Brian stepped out of his shoes, pulled his sweater over his head and unzipped his jeans. "Where do you want me?" he asked, fighting off an almost overwhelming need to close his eyes as he stripped down to pale-blue boxer shorts.

At the sight of his near naked body, Beth felt as if she'd been struck dumb. She couldn't take her eyes off him. Each one of those glorious muscles was a tribute to her skill and his perseverance. She felt a ridiculous surge of pride at the accomplishment. More than anything, she wanted to run her fingers over his smooth, bronzed flesh and prove to herself that he really was as perfect as he looked.

With that thought in mind, she glanced over at his king-size bed and her imagination ran amuck. He would lie down on the cream-colored sheets. She would stroke him, caress him and that would lead to . . .

"Beth?"

She jumped at the sound of his voice. "What?"

"Do you want to do this on the bed or the floor?"

"What?"

Brian couldn't help it. As exhausted as he was, he still had to chuckle. The guilty look on her face, the shimmering gold in her eyes, told him exactly what she'd been thinking. "Ah, Beth, if only we could. The spirit is willing, but the flesh is weak."

"I . . . I never said . . . I'm sorry if you think . . ."

A knowing smile touched his lips and his eyes twinkled as he broke into her disjointed effort to escape what he was saying. "Don't apologize. Knowing you want me is the nicest homecoming present you could have given me. Forgive me if I don't take you up on the offer until I'm able to give you something more than a pleasant lunch in return. I promise. You won't have to wait long."

"I'm not waiting."

"Aren't you?"

Even though they both knew that she was looking at him "that way," she said, "Brian, I didn't come here thinking we would make love."

"It doesn't matter," he retorted, lips twitching. "You'll leave here knowing we did."

Was this really happening? It was. Did Brian really plan to make love to her before she left his apartment? He did. What about Melinda? Where did she fit into this scenario? Beth didn't intend to ask for fear he might tell her. This new Brian disconcerted her, being blunt when she'd have much preferred him to keep his explicit thoughts to himself. Once she had admired his openness and honesty. Now it made her extremely nervous.

She could see that the only way to salvage any semblance of dignity in this situation was to take what he said in good grace and pray he didn't say anything else. She didn't think she could handle any more references to what might occur in the very near future. And *might*, she wanted to point out to him, was the operative word, no matter what he thought.

"Well, one thing you won't have to wait for any longer is your massage," she managed spiritedly. "Let's use the floor. I can get better leverage there than on the bed."

"I'll keep that in mind for future reference," Brian teased with a yawn as he lowered himself to the wide bath towel she'd spread out for him on the carpet. Turning his head to one side, he stretched his long body, closed his eyes and sighed. "I've been looking forward to this for so long."

Eyes averted from his lithe form, Beth knelt down beside him and opened her bag. With a wry smile, she rejected the camphorated oil she'd intended to use on him in favor of an almond-scented lotion. Determined to treat him as one of her patients, she poured some lotion into her hands and set to work on the tight muscles of his shoulders and neck. The man who said he'd looked forward to her massage for so long was asleep within seconds.

Beth continued her efforts to the accompaniment of his gentle snores and appreciative sighs. Within moments, it became obvious that she wasn't the one who needed to be concerned over losing her virtue. Brian was completely oblivious to her ministrations, while she was aware of every breath he took, every movement of his beautiful near naked body, and she wanted him so badly that she was shaking.

She was supremely grateful that he wasn't aware of her actions on a conscious level. Otherwise he would have known the exact second her traitorous fingers stopped kneading and started caressing. He would have been aware that she continued to stroke him long after the massage she had promised was done, that she couldn't seem to stop touching him in all the ways she'd imagined doing when he'd first stripped off his clothes.

Eventually, however, Beth realized that if she kept on doing what she was doing he was going to wake up. From what he'd said before falling asleep, if he opened his eyes and found her staring so adoringly at him, her hands all over him, he would take immediate action. Until she knew exactly where she stood in his life, she couldn't let that happen.

Neither could she resist kissing him. Bending over him, she touched his lips with her own, barely able to suppress a small moan as his lips parted beneath hers. No! She warned silently, pulling back. She had to resist temptation.

With a troubled sigh, Beth began placing her supplies back in her bag. Then, trying not to make a sound, she got to her feet and walked over to the bed. She stripped off a blanket and very carefully retraced her steps. Brian hadn't moved a muscle.

After one last lingering look at his sleeping form, she covered him with the blanket and left before she could change her mind.

"Damn!" Brian picked himself up off the floor and, without stopping to pull on his pants, charged for the door. In the darkness he misjudged the distance and stubbed his toe on the corner of his bed. The sharp pain that shot up his leg fostered a much more profane curse, but didn't halt his passage to the living room.

Just as he thought, it was empty, as were the dining room and kitchen. "Well, what did you expect, fool?" he questioned out loud as he stomped back into the living room and switched on the lamp nearest the couch.

Judging by the view out the windows it was well after dusk. Streetlights were on all over the city. He glared at the wall clock. It was almost midnight. "Damn it to hell! You not only slept away the whole blasted day but half the night."

Seething with frustration, he planted himself in front of the smoked glass. Hands on hips, he stared out at the glittering skyline and willed himself to calm down. He'd blown it! Really blown it! He should have known when he got off the plane that he wasn't up to seeing Beth right away. But did he listen to the dictates of his weary body? No.

Fool that he was, he'd talked himself into believing that he couldn't wait even one more day to have her back in his arms where she belonged. Therefore, instead of sweeping her away on a sensual tide, he'd proved conclusively that he was the same pigheaded nitwit she'd left behind a year before. As always, he'd ignored his body's limitations and gone along with the ill-fated plan conceived by his feeble brain.

Well, he'd certainly made his bed, but Beth wasn't lying in it and he had no one to blame for that but himself. "So what are you going to do about it, Towers?"

He still didn't have the answer as he stood under the shower. Nor later, when he pulled on a pair of brown cords and a beige cable-knit sweater. During the elevator ride down from the penthouse, nothing came to mind, and he didn't have a clue as to what he was going to say as he slid behind the wheel of his silver Jaguar.

He had no trouble finding a parking spot in front of Beth's building, but the light in his brain didn't come on until he'd been sitting there for over an hour. His days as a high school quarterback might be over, but he'd learned a few aggressive tactics that had served him well even after he'd switched from passing to receiving in college. In order to win the game, the quarterback had to lead the offense with relentless fervor, rely on some fancy footwork and, if all else failed, put his future on the line with an all or nothing pass.

His quarterbacking skills might be a bit rusty, but what was lacking in experience could be more than made up for by enthusiasm. With a sound mental attitude and a well-executed game plan, he couldn't help but be victorious. In the face of his offensive strategy, Beth didn't stand a chance.

Brian got out of the car, the confident expression on his face never wavering until he saw Beth's name printed on the row of mailboxes inside the front door of her building. His anxiety continued to build as he sprinted up the stairs to the third floor. By the time he was standing before her door, preparing to knock, he'd broken out in a cold sweat and his stomach had tied itself into knots.

"So what if this idea doesn't work," he chided himself as he pounded on the thick wood. "There's always begging."

When the door finally opened, he was presented with a feminine vision dressed in a graphically disturbing, thigh high pink T-shirt.

"Brian?"

Brian groaned inwardly, staring at the enticing outline of her body. How was he supposed to pretend to be angry with a woman who looked so damned soft and sexy that all he wanted to do was scoop her up in his arms and carry her back to bed? It was obvious that was where she had been. Her cheeks were flushed a delicate pink, her hair was a wild caramel-colored tangle and her dark eyes were dreamy.

He cleared his throat and belatedly remembered his hastily conceived game plan. If he wanted to join her under the covers, he had to take the offense first thing. Pasting an irritated expression on his face, he inquired, "Are you deliberately trying to drive me crazy? What the hell are you doing here? Why didn't you wake me if you wanted to leave? You'd better have a good explanation for this, Beth Crosby!"

"I'd better have a . . . Drive *you* crazy?" Beth gasped in befuddlement as Brian pushed past her, his face dark as a thundercloud.

"Now you wait just a minute, Brian Towers!" She slammed the door closed and whirled around to find that he'd already plopped himself down on her couch. His arms were folded over his chest, and his expression dared her to dispute his right to be where he was.

"Well!"

The last foggy residue of sleep that had hampered Beth's thinking was abruptly dispelled by an arousing spurt of temper. "You've got some nerve charging in here in the middle of the night, making wild accusations. You're the one who owes me an explanation."

"You know damned well why I'm here," Brian shot back, something in his eyes giving her a hint that he wasn't nearly as angry as he looked. But when he spoke again that thought was obliterated from her mind.

"I told you what was supposed to happen when I woke up from my nap," he reminded her. "I've thought of little else but making love to you for the past two weeks, and when I wake up it's pitch-black outside and you're gone. How do you think I felt?"

His blue eyes were accusing, his voice thick with frustration. "You wanted me just as much as I wanted you, but did you give me time to regain my strength? No, you just walked out without even saying goodbye. What kind of a woman would do that to a man?"

Beth's mouth fell open with shock at his conceited estimation of himself and their situation. She slumped back against the door, so stunned she felt weak. According to Brian, she was supposed to have waited around in his apartment all day and all night like some harem girl dancing attendance while his highness recovered enough strength to make love to her. If nothing else, Brian had certainly gained a colossal nerve in the past year!

Well, she'd gained a few things, too, and one of them was a free lesson in karate. She might not have learned enough to do any real bodily harm to him, but she was confident about her next move. Brian Towers was about to be chopped off at the knees. Eyes fired green with self-righteous anger, she marched toward the couch.

Brian watched her coming, remembering the last time he'd seen that murderous look in her eyes. He'd forgotten her vicious response to unwarranted attacks, but his memory was fast returning.

Provoking her anger had been a bad idea. Getting down on his knees and begging would have been much better. Much better, he decided as he heard her pronounce, "Out! Get out of here right now!"

"Uh . . . Beth . . . I don't think I've gone about this the right way." Brian pressed himself back against the soft floral cushions, crossing his forearms in front of his face in case she turned violent. "All I wanted—"

"I know what you wanted, you jackass, but I don't come to heel when a man snaps his fingers. Now I suggest you get out of here while you still have fingers left to snap."

Brian chuckled, half in admiration, half in self-derision. "You'd do it, too. You'd really hurt me."

"You'd better believe it, cowboy."

"I believe it," he muttered in a resigned tone that made her think he meant to cause her no more trouble. Hanging his head, he peered sheepishly up at her through his dark lashes. "I apologize for my thoroughly detestable behavior this evening. I was way out of line. Forgive me?"

Beth sniffed, wishing he wasn't wearing that beleaguered expression that made him appear so boyish and vulnerable. "You were out of line," she acknowledged more to herself than to him. "And detestable."

Brian nodded. "And you more than deserve an explanation."

Her eyes remained wary. "Yes I do."

"Will you sit down here and listen to me for a second?"

Beth eyed the couch and the humble pose of the man who was beseeching her to join him on it. Sensing a trap, she stalled. "I can hear you perfectly well from up here."

"Will you at least drop your defenses a little? I'll admit I'm a jackass, but a poor, dumb beast like me doesn't deserve to be horsewhipped for behaving in character. A little browbeating, maybe . . ."

Try as she might, Beth couldn't prevent her lips from quirking in amusement. "Browbeating definitely," she agreed. Much surer of him in this mood, she condescended to sit down on the far end of the couch as Brian pleaded for permission to explain himself. "Okay. What was this all about?"

Brian closed his eyes for a second, let out a long sigh, then sat forward with his head down and his forearms resting on his knees. "When I woke up tonight, I realized that feeling your soft beautiful hands running all over my body had just been a figment of my overactive imagination. You were gone, had been gone for hours. I'd never been so frustrated in my life. I felt like such a fool for falling asleep on you like that, so I—"

"So you came over here to relieve your frustration," she concluded sarcastically.

Brian cast her a quelling look from beneath one raised brow. "Do you want me to tell my side or don't you?"

"Well, didn't you?"

"No, I didn't," Brian stated bluntly, not quite able to hide his rising irritation. "I masterminded this plan, stupid I'll admit, but—"

"You actually thought you could waltz in here, growl at me for your frustration and I'd jump right into bed with you?" Beth asked incredulously. "What kind of women have you been hanging out with lately, Brian?"

"Damn it! I'm trying to bare my soul here, Beth. It would be polite of you to listen without interruption."

"After this I don't know why you expect me to be polite," she maintained piously. Folding her arms over her breasts, she lifted her chin, unaware of the jealous sparkle in her eyes as she continued snidely, "Maybe

Melinda Graham dotes on your every word, but any man who wants my undivided attention has to earn it."

"Like Jeff Samuels?" Brian retorted, his own jealousy coming to the fore. "Has he earned your undivided attention?"

"Don't by silly." From the look in Brian's eyes when he'd posed the question, Beth had no doubt what he meant by undivided attention. In a scathing tone, she set him straight. "Jeff and I are friends. No more, no less."

"Melly and I date back to diapers," Brian matched her tone. "As any good friend would do, I've been holding her hand through a painful divorce. What's your excuse?"

"My excuse for what?"

"For letting Samuels hang all over you?" Brian snarled. Tossing off his abject pose, he slid across the cushions. He captured her chin between his thumb and finger and gibed, "You forget, I was watching the two of you dancing together the night of the auction. He couldn't keep his hands off you."

Beth pulled her chin out of his grasp. "As I recall, I had far more problems with your hands that night than with his!"

"Is that so?"

"Yes, it is!"

Several more seconds went by as each of them pondered what the other had just said. Nose to nose, blue eyes glared into hazel. Fists clenched and unclenched.

Chins lifted in challenge before the lights came on in their brains.

Brian revealed the first glimmers of a smile. His lips curved slightly upward, widened to a dumbfounded smirk and finally parted in a full-fledged grin. "So what's our problem?"

He was so close that Beth could feel his breath on her lips. His beautiful eyes were focused on the elusive dimple in her cheek and she couldn't help herself. She allowed him to see it just before she murmured softly, "You've become a high-handed, dictatorial potentate."

"No, I haven't," Brian negated huskily. "I'm a desperate man who's been waiting without you far too long." He pulled her down on him as he fell back on the cushions. "Far, far too long."

Beth wasn't given the chance to speak as his fingers came up beneath the hair of her nape and he brought her face down to his. His mouth was urgent, demanding and sweet. The taste of him, the feel of him, was something she'd wanted for so long she had no thought of denying herself or him. Lips parted, she waited for the hungry probe of his tongue and moaned in satisfaction when it came.

Starving for each other, they moved to discard all barriers. Beth's T-shirt was disposed of with one upward sweep of Brian's arm, and his clothes, though more difficult to remove, suffered a similar fate. At last, both naked, they arched toward each other in a frantic effort to absorb all they could at one time.

Bodies locked together in a frenzy of need, they sought to recapture the joy they had felt only one other time in their lives and had feared they would never feel again. Beth gloried in the knowledge that Brian's body was burning up with her touch, his flesh so hot it seared her palms. She loved him and showed him the power of that emotion with her hands, her lips, with every part of her body.

Brian turned her head to his mouth, molding her body to the uncontrolled thrusting of his hips. As she had done the last time, she was giving him everything, making it impossible for him to do anything but surrender himself to the pleasure. His tongue thrust inside her, savoring her sweetness; his body demanded he give in to an even greater craving. He pulled back just in time.

"This is crazy," Brian rasped, barely able to think as the throbbing in his loins mounted to painful intensity. He didn't want to take her on the floor. He wanted to savor every moment of this in a normal setting—a bed. The first time they'd made love on the hard, bare ground. A floor wasn't much of an improvement. "I'm not going to let this happen again," he vowed.

Caught up in her own raging senses, Beth barely heard him and didn't understand what he was saying. "Brian," she breathed his name against the golden hairs that curled on his chest. "I want you. I want you," she chanted, alternating the fevered words with the litany of kisses she was pressing across his hard, bronzed flesh. Legs entwined with his, her lips continued along the route of crisp hair that arrowed down to his navel, her breasts brushing against him, forging the way.

At the first touch of her mouth on him, Brian groaned as if in fierce pain. Beth looked up just before his hands descended with a death grip on her arms. "What's wrong?" she whispered.

Brian sat up, hauling her onto his lap as he drew in a shuddering breath. "No more," he ground out between clenched teeth, pressing her face to his chest as he fought to regain the control he'd nearly lost.

Confused and hurt, Beth stiffened in his arms and tried to pull away, but the harder she pulled the tighter he held her. "Let me go," she demanded, humiliated by his rejection.

"Not on your life!" Brian vowed, lifting her high against his chest as he stood up from the couch.

Ignoring the squirming body in his arms, he strode toward the bedroom, but rejected that idea as soon as he saw the size of the bed. "Well, that's not going to work. We won't have much more room there than we had on the couch."

Realizing that what could have happened on the plush carpeting of his bedroom was about to transpire on the soft, blue pile of hers made him laugh. "It seems we're fated to do this thing without making use of the normal conventions. But one of these days, sweetheart, we're going to make love on a common, ordinary bed like normal, everyday people."

Beth couldn't believe that he'd halted their lovemaking because he'd found the location uncomfortable. Obviously his feelings for her didn't transcend time and place as hers did for him. She hadn't been aware of anything but her need for him and would have been perfectly content if things had progressed to their natural conclusion without benefit of a spacious mattress. The fact that such an inconsequential thing mattered to him—mattered enough that he could pull away from her in the midst of their rising passion—made her doubt the rightness of their coming together at all.

She stated as much as soon as he lowered her onto the carpet and came down beside her. "This is happening much too fast, Brian. I—"

Beth's words were cut off by a finger pressed over her lips. "No," he denied ardently, leaning over her as he stared down into her face. "This is going to be slow. I swore if I ever got the chance to make love to you again, I'd show some self-control."

A dull flush stained his cheeks as he berated himself. "I don't know what happens to me when I'm with you. . . ." His gaze traveled down the curves of her breasts to her long shapely legs and back up to the soft, curling hair at the juncture of her thighs. "Yes, I do. But this time, I refuse to give in to my own pleasure until you've had all you can take."

Blue eyes glittering with blazing passion and grim determination, he growled, "This time will be different, Beth, I promise you."

"Is that what you...why you?" Beth was shocked by the misconception he'd adopted about the first time they'd made love. "Brian, how could you think that I didn't enjoy myself as much as you did? I'll never forget that day as long as I live. It was beautiful, so very, very beautiful."

"You were beautiful. I was a slathering half-wit." Brian shifted his legs, inserting one thigh between hers but keeping most of his weight off her by propping his arms on either side of her head. "So desperate to make you mine, I couldn't wait to be certain it was just as perfect for you."

Beth attempted to pull him down on her, anxious to reassure him, but he shook his head and arched away from her outstretched arms. "It was perfect, Brian," she insisted. "It couldn't have been more perfect."

"Yes, it could," he maintained, and proceeded to demonstrate.

She was lost in the feel and taste of his mouth on her mouth, on her throat, on the valley between her breasts. It became more and more difficult to breath as he molded his palms to her breasts and fit himself between her thighs. While his fingers stroked and caressed her, his lips closed over one nipple, then the other, until both were throbbing.

It was she who feared losing control as he left her quivering breasts to kiss his way down her body. She gasped in shocked pleasure as his lips found her, adored her, tormented her. She ached for release, her body on fire, her delicate flesh so sensitized by the rasp of his tongue, the tantalizing nibbles of his teeth and the caressing movements of his lips that she pleaded with him to stop, knowing she would die if he did.

Brian wanted her so badly that he felt he might explode. At the same time, he couldn't get enough of watching her arch higher and higher with the sensations he was inciting. She went wild with each kiss and when he brought his fingers into play, she went over the edge before he could join her. Nothing could have prepared him for the feelings that came over him as he heard her cry out his name. In that moment, he knew he would never love another woman.

He pulled her against him, holding her until the violent shudders were spent. When they were over, she opened her eyes and gazed up at him with such adoration, he was momentarily blinded. And then, suddenly, it was she who was holding him, pushing his shoulders down on the carpet as she took the dominant position.

Braced for the onslaught he knew he couldn't withstand for any length of time, but hoping to remain strong long enough for her to grow hungry again, Brian was stunned when she immediately took him inside her. With the slightest motion of her hips, the slightest tension of her thighs, he experienced wave upon wave of intensifying pleasure.

"No," he groaned, trying to hold back, but she denied him that option, going with him as he rolled to the side. Drawing him deeper and deeper inside her with each undulation of her hips, Beth wrapped both arms around his waist. He couldn't stop it, stop her as she tried to show there was no reason for further restraint.

"Come with me, Brian," she murmured, but he was too far gone to show he understood. After that, came ecstasy that was no greater for one than the other. They weathered the shock waves together, and when it was over, they were clasped together like the sole survivors of a maelstrom.

When he could manage it, Brian rolled onto his back to stare blankly up at the swirling white paint on her ceiling. Finally the question he wanted to ask made the journey from his dazed brain to his lips. "Beth?"

"Mmmm?" she asked, unable to form a more intelligible response.

"You know this was right, don't you?"

"Uh-huh."

"And you're willing to admit that what we feel just might last for... for a very long time?"

"Yes."

Brian let out the breath he'd been holding as he waited for her answer. So relieved was he by the one she gave, it took him a long time to recover. "So what's the next step?"

After a long pause, Beth replied, "I guess we try to get reacquainted and make sure we're still friends."

"Friends!" Brian sat up, oblivious to her nakedness and his own as he queried incredulously. "You want us to be friends?"

"It would be nice." Beth nodded as she brought her legs beneath her and pushed herself up with her arms. With a mischievous smile on her lips, she scooted across the distance between them and settled herself on his lap. She gave a blissful sigh, then turned her face into his broad shoulder.

"Since we already know what great lovers we are," she observed as her mouth began moving over his skin, "I think we should explore all the other aspects of a lasting relationship."

"I'm all for exploring," Brian agreed in a choked tone as Beth showed him the path to vast new regions of discovery.

11

"YOU CAN LICK THIS THING," Brian persuaded. He gently cradled a limp hand in his palm. "Come on back to the world. There's so much you'll miss if you don't. Football season's in full swing, buddy, and our Buckeyes are leading the Big Ten. I've got a fifty-yard-line seat waiting for you as soon as you're on your feet."

Brian kept up the one-sided conversation as he sat at the bedside of the sixteen-year-old boy. Four weeks ago, Jerry Liebermann had been injured in a car accident. The broken bones were healing, but the youth was still in a state of semicoma.

It had been only a couple of days since he had last visited Jerry, but Brian was sure he detected some improvment. The boy's lashes seemed to flutter more frequently, as if he were trying hard to open them. And wasn't his grip just a little stronger? God, he hoped so.

As if it were yesterday, he could remember his own struggle up through the foggy mire that was coma. His return had occurred in slow stages; at first he'd heard snatches of conversation and had brief moments of awareness that slipped away quickly. Gradually, the sounds had become clearer, made more sense, and finally he'd awakened to full consciousness. And to a new horror—he hadn't been able to move a muscle.

Fortunately for the young man lying in the bed—one arm in a plaster cast and one leg wrapped to the hip in a stabilizer—the prognosis was better than it had been for Brian. Jerry sometimes turned his head from side to side, moaned softly, moved his good leg restlessly and was able to return the squeeze of a hand occasionally. When he awakened, especially if that happened soon, he would probably display little or no neurological damage.

Brian realized he'd been incredibly lucky that his brain had returned to normal function. As this boy did, he'd had the constant support of a loving family. While his mother had been the unfailing source of optimism when he'd been locked in, it had been his father who had understood and supported him through the rough moments of that first year after his return to the world.

While he chattered on to Jerry, he thought back to the first time he'd worked up the courage to attend an Ohio State football game. At the first-quarter break, Hadley had suggested they walk down to the concession stands to "stretch our legs a bit."

They'd stretched their legs all right, Brian remembered wryly. They'd walked out of the stadium and a good two miles along the Olentangey River that bordered the campus. His father hadn't said anything, just walked along companionably beside him. Brian didn't know what he would have done without his father that day, and many others.

They hadn't returned to the game that day, but they'd gone back the following week and the next, and every Saturday afternoon the Buckeyes were playing at home. Each time it had gotten easier and they'd stayed longer. That this was something Brian had to do was an unspoken understanding between them. Hadley had offered the kind of support only a father could give, and he'd been there at every hurdle Brian had had to conquer.

After having spent so much time in virtual isolation, any gathering of more than a handful of people had been difficult for Brian. The first inkling he'd had that crowds might be a problem for him had been at his "coming out" celebration. As long as he'd stayed on the patio he'd been able to handle it; inside had been a different story.

Never far from his side, his father had sensed his anxiety and adroitly whisked him to quieter surroundings. As the months had gone by, Brian had grown accustomed to having people around him again, and finally, crowds were no longer a problem. Brian knew his father hadn't discussed either of these adjustment problems with his mother. They'd shared the knowledge and dealt with things together as best they could. Consequently they'd forged a stronger bond between them than ever before.

The sound of a door swishing open behind him didn't stop Brian's persistent enticement and coaxing of Jerry. "Show me that grip again, pal." He waited patiently as the once strong fingers moved and tightened weakly around his.

"That's it, cowboy," he complimented enthusiastically, and felt another slight squeeze on his fingers.

"You're going to be up and at 'em in no time. You be sure to give your mom a good squeeze when she gets here. Moms need things like that. Don't forget your dad, either."

Beth stepped into the room and came up to stand behind Brian's chair. Unable to help herself, she wrapped her arms around his shoulders and gave him a squeeze of her own. She'd known about his visits to the coma patients at the center and some of the hospitals in town, but this was the first time she'd been witness to the special brand of therapy only he could give.

She wasn't surprised to discover how gentle and reassuring he was to this young man who, for all his size, was probably very frightened. Brian had been there. He understood. He hadn't been that much older when he'd been in the same condition. And Brian's fears had been no less than Jerry's.

Of the many facets of the complex man he'd become Beth loved his compassion the most. He could be so understanding, so sensitive and give so generously of himself. A willingness—maybe even a need—to help others was something she and Brian shared.

Brian closed his free hand over Beth's. "Jerry," he continued addressing the inert figure on the bed. "A foxy lady has come in to work with you. Her name is Beth and she once helped me a lot. She kept my muscles in condition when I couldn't do it myself. She can do the same for you.

"She's got soft hands and very nice—" He wiggled his shoulders against Beth's breasts. She caught her breath and mentally crossed her fingers as she waited for Brian to finish his statement. "Eyes," he supplied, then added, "and a beautiful face. You'd better open those eyes of yours soon so you can see her, but I'm warning you to keep your hands to yourself. I saw her first."

After a few more parting comments and a promise to be back the next day, Brian let go of Jerry's hand and stood up. "You take good care of my buddy here, Beth," he said for Jerry's benefit as he curled his arms around her.

Holding her lightly, Brian bent his head until his lips brushed her ear. "And I'll take good care of you later tonight," he promised in a low whisper that sent a tremor all the way to her toes. And then he was gone.

Beth had to take several deep breaths before she could gain control of her senses and quiet her rioting pulse. Brian did take good care of her. After three weeks, he knew every sensitive spot on her body and how to best tend every one.

"Well, Jerry, I've got my orders," she said breathlessly as she advanced on her patient.

All through the therapy session with Jerry, Beth kept up a nonstop conversation, but a part of her mind was centered on Brian and the upcoming evening. Glenda and Hadley had just returned from a month-long cruise, and Beth and Brian were having dinner with them at the Towerses' home. It would be the first time Beth had stepped foot in that house since she'd left there over a year ago.

Though she'd occasionally heard from both Glenda and Hadley over the past months, Beth had mixed feelings about this evening. On the one hand, she was looking forward to seeing them again. They were delightful people. On the other, she wasn't quite sure what kind of role she would now play in their lives. Once she'd been their son's therapist—an employee. They'd treated her like an honored friend, yes, but she'd been an employee just the same.

Now her association with Brian and his family wasn't so clearly defined. Or maybe it was. She was Brian's current woman. Whether they would see her as anything more was probably wishful thinking on her part. In truth, she had no basis for believing she was anything else to Brian. Though their relationship had quickly escalated to intimacy, there had been no further mention of permanency, and no declaration of love.

She had asked for time to reestablish their friendship and Brian had given it to her. He was courting her smoothly, urbanely and maturely. He'd taken her to dinner at some of the smartest clubs in town. They'd gone dancing. Their engagements had been varied, running from the casualness of a Saturday-afternoon football game to the gala season opening of the Columbus Symphony.

Beth couldn't deny that he'd become experienced in the arts of pleasing a woman on every plane. He was everything any woman would want and Beth was no exception.

In bed she became a wanton woman who couldn't get enough of him. Indeed, the physical side of their relationship couldn't have been any better. But Beth wondered if Brian's feelings ran as deeply as they once had. She couldn't help but think he was holding something back. Although she knew he had the highest regard for her, he had never intimated that their affair would become anything more than it was.

For what remained of her workday, Beth speculated on Brian's motives for inviting her to a family dinner, and whether Glenda and Hadley might read anything into it. "They're probably used to his bringing female guests to dinner by now," she muttered as she pulled her car into the apartment house parking lot. "From what I read in the papers, he's dated scores of women in the past year. I'm just the latest."

That last declaration brought her full circle. No matter how she looked at it, she was Brian's current woman. He was twenty-six, and though Beth was sure his parents hoped he would one day marry and have a family, she doubted they looked upon every woman he brought to the house as a future daughter-in-law. Even if he hadn't lost five important years of his life, he wouldn't be feeling any pressure to settle down yet.

"Just enjoy the evening as a gathering of old friends," Beth told herself over and over again as she showered and went through her closet. The dress she chose was comfortable, but it was also one of the most complimentary she'd ever owned. The rust color of the soft, lightweight wool brought out the auburn highlights in her hair, flattered her complexion and emphasized the warm colors in her hazel eyes. The lines were basic, a simple sheath belted lightly at her waist, long sleeves and a vee neck where she'd tucked a paisley scarf of ivory, jade and rust. The dress flattered her figure, hinting at the curves beneath and revealing a goodly length of shapely leg with the slit at one side.

She was gratified by Brian's low whistle when she opened the door. "Hello, gorgeous," he drawled, his gaze sweeping down her body and back up to her face.

Burying his fingers in the silken waves that framed her face, he cradled her head in his palms, then brought his mouth down on hers. Slowly and deliberately he conquered every crevice of her sweet mouth. Soon, though, the questing exploration of his tongue became more urgent, the pulsing thrusts sending unmistakable messages.

Trembling with the force of her need, Beth clutched at Brian's shoulders for support. Dropping one hand to her waist, he pulled her into the strength of his body, then slid his palm around to her back and lower. Blending her curves with his planes, he left her with no doubt as to how quickly his own desire had flared. His hard maleness throbbed against her, and Beth couldn't help it when her hips writhed against him. Her reaction elicited a low moan from deep within Brian's throat.

"Let's get this evening over with," he said in a rough whisper. Planting a quick kiss on her lips, he set her away from him. His smile was rueful as he looked at the fullness of her mouth and the smear of brick-red lipstick that went beyond its outline. "Uh . . . you might want to go make some repairs."

Reaching up, Beth ran her thumb along his lips. "So might you," she returned teasingly, holding her thumb up to show the smudge of red she'd brushed from his mouth. "Unless you're into wearing lipstick these days."

"Only yours," he assured her as she turned away and started back to her bedroom to restore her makeup.

"Wrong shade for you," she called through the doorway.

It's the right shade if it's your shade. Taking out his handkerchief, Brian rubbed away the evidence of their kiss. He studied the streak of red on the white cloth for a moment before replacing the handkerchief in his pocket.

He'd been wiping that particular shade of lipstick off his mouth a lot in the past few weeks. It was impossible for him not to begin each evening they spent together with a kiss. Each time he came to her apartment, it took an heroic effort to keep from canceling their plans for the evening. All he ever wanted to do was sweep her up in his arms and carry her off to make love to her.

He consoled himself with the knowledge that this evening would end that way. The only blemish on that idyllic image was that he would have to leave her at some point in the early hours, a departure that was becoming more and more difficult. One of these days he wouldn't be able to help himself and he'd blurt out his feelings, demanding that she marry him before he went stark, raving mad.

"GREAT DINNER, MOM," Brian complimented as he pushed himself away from the table.

"Thank you, dear, but I can't take credit for all of it," Glenda admitted. Looking down the long table, she smiled at her husband. "I only made the dessert and salad. Your father prepared the lamb and everything else."

A smile teased the corners of his mouth as Brian drawled, "Really? Feeling sorry for Mom since the cook's still on vacation, or did you pick up a few new skills on the cruise, Dad?"

"Not on the cruise," Hadley quickly corrected, rising from his chair and gesturing that they should adjourn to the living room. "I always liked to cook. I just have more time, now that I don't have to run Towers Enterprises all by myself."

"And you're a much better cook than I am, darling. Working together in the kitchen reminded me of the first years of our marriage when we lived in the little house and your father was still running the corporation," Glenda said whimsically while Hadley pulled out her chair.

Always the considerate hostess, Glenda turned to Beth as they walked through the foyer and explained, "When Hadley and I were first married we lived in what is now the farm manager's house. Hadley was running the farms, so it was the logical place for us to live. Part of the house was the original Towers homestead. Brian's grandfather always referred to it as the little house."

Having seen the sprawling farmhouse, Beth wouldn't have called it "little." Glenda's next words echoed her thoughts. "It always seemed a bit silly to call it the 'little' house. The place has twelve rooms."

Hadley smiled fondly down at his wife, seated on one of the two love seats flanking the fireplace in the living room. Dropping a hand to her shoulder, he said, "We didn't use too many of those rooms, did we, dear?"

Glenda returned the smile, covering his hand with hers. Her eyes twinkled, while her cheeks grew a trifle rosy. "No, I guess we didn't," she finally replied. "But, then, we really didn't need much."

"Just each other," Hadley supplied.

For a long moment, Hadley and Glenda gazed at each other as if they were the only two people in the room...possibly the world. It was clear that they were still very much in love after three decades of marriage. Beth envied their happiness and the years they had shared.

Once Brian had looked at her in the same way, though his adoring gaze had not been based on memories but an imagined future. However, it would seem that the year's separation had killed the purity of the love he had offered her. Now? His eyes upon her could only be described as hot and hungry.

"One of the best parts about living in the little house was that we were all alone," Hadley remarked, sitting down beside Glenda and stretching his arm along the back of the couch. "Too bad it's not available anymore."

"Why? You thinking about exchanging your three-piece suits for overalls, Dad?" Brian asked from the sideboard, where he was pouring liqueurs.

Hadley shook his head, a slight look of regret in his eyes. "No, I've grown far too soft to be an active farmer again. As soon as I can turn over the reins of Towers Enterprises to you, son, I'm going to retire and bounce my grandchildren on my knee."

Brian set the small silver tray down on the cocktail table with enough force to make the crystal glasses rattle. Startled, Beth looked up and saw the quelling scowl he sent his father. The look was brief, and by the time Brian faced her, he was smiling again. If a few drops of the amber liqueur hadn't spilled onto the tray, Beth would have thought she'd imagined Brian's show of displeasure at Hadley's mention of grandchildren.

"I shouldn't think you'd be turning the company over any too soon," Glenda interposed, placing the emphasis on Brian's taking over the company. "Brian's been with the company less than a year. Give him a little time before you drop all that responsibility in his lap."

Despite Glenda's smooth interjection, Hadley still looked puzzled and embarrassed. Beth was sure he had attached the same interpretation to Brian's reaction as she had. For the first time during the evening Beth felt uncomfortable, very much an intruder in this family gathering.

Unlike the delicate crystal that had survived Brian's anger, her own hopes of rekindling the love he had once professed to have for her had finally shattered. His thoughts were as clear as if he'd spoken them aloud. *This is not the time nor the company to be mentioning grandchildren. I have no plans with this woman to supply them for you.*

Clearing his throat, Hadley addressed his wife's statement. "Well, of course, dear. I didn't mean I expected to retire next month, or even next year. I was merely describing how I intend to spend that retirement." He gave her shoulders an affectionate squeeze. "It'll also give me more time to spend with you. Maybe we can take a world cruise."

Glenda laughed. Winking at Brian and Beth, she teased, "He's only saying that now that he's safely back on solid ground. Hadley's favorite part of the cruise was stopping at all the islands."

"I must admit I was very glad Greece has so many," Hadley divulged. "After the first day on that ship, I discovered I'm not much of a sailor."

Though Beth was included in the conversation that followed, she still felt like an outsider. Glenda and Hadley were as warm and friendly toward her as they had always been. Brian, seated beside her on the other love seat, had draped his arm along the back, his hand often brushing her shoulder or her nape. It was a cozy, familial evening.

Beth, however, wasn't a member of this family. She'd been Brian's therapist, the woman whose skills had been needed to keep him fit and ready for the life he had returned to. Back then, she had fulfilled a need in his life, a temporary need. For all she knew, she was doing the same thing again.

When she'd first been hired by Glenda, Beth hadn't known how long the job would last, or what the ultimate result of her efforts would be. There didn't appear to be any more certainty in her renewed relationship with Brian. The only certainty was that she loved him, and by all indications, her love was not returned.

Realizing she'd been so lost in introspection she hadn't been contributing much to the conversation, Beth asked if the Towerses had taken any pictures during their trip.

"Rolls and rolls of film," Glenda answered gaily.

Brian slumped lower on the sofa and groaned, but Beth sent him a quick frown and enthused, "We'd love to see them."

"How sweet of you, Beth," Glenda responded. "But I refuse to punish you for your politeness. There's nothing worse than having to sift through hundreds of snapshots of somebody else's trip. It was nice of you two to come all the way out here and welcome us back, but surely you have something far more exciting to do with the rest of your evening."

"She's kicking us out," Brian informed Beth with a grin. Standing, he reached for her hand and tugged her up beside him.

"Of course I'm not kicking you out." Glenda feigned an affronted air. "I was providing you with a graceful exit so you wouldn't have to continue to pretend interest."

"We *were* interested!" Beth and Brian protested simultaneously.

"Did you practice that duet?" Hadley quipped, shaking Brian's outstretched hand, then leaning forward and kissing Beth's cheek. "Glenda's right. Run along. Frankly, I'm tired. Haven't gotten used to Ohio time yet." As if to reinforce his statement he yawned.

A few minutes later, Brian was handing Beth into the low-slung Jaguar he'd left parked by the front entrance. "They really needed that trip," he remarked. Putting the car into gear, he started down the drive.

"They look more rested and happier than I've ever seen them," Beth replied, wishing her mind would stop replaying that one moment during the evening when Brian had reacted so furiously to his father. "It was wonderful being with them again." She crossed her legs and settled closer to the door, unconsciously putting as much distance between Brian and her as possible.

"They were equally glad to see you."

"Your parents are two of the most gracious people I've ever met."

"So why did you suddenly start looking so sad?"

Lulled by the desultory comments they'd been making, Beth was caught off guard by Brian's question. She turned her head sharply toward him. Even in the darkness, she could see the searching look in his eyes before he turned his attention back to the road.

When she didn't immediately answer, he elaborated on his query. "Everything was fine. You seemed to be enjoying yourself. Then suddenly, right after we moved into the living room, you looked as if you'd just lost your best friend."

I may have lost more than that. "I didn't mean to give that impression. Like your father, I guess I'm just a little tired."

Reaching across the gearshift, Brian plucked Beth's hand from her lap. He brought it to his lips and kissed her knuckles, then proceeded to suckle each of her fingertips in turn. "I know just the thing for a tired woman."

"An early bedtime."

Brian chuckled deep in his chest and pressed a kiss to her palm. "I like the way your mind works, woman."

Beth pulled her hand from Brian and replaced it with its mate in her lap. "That's not what I had in mind," she snapped, instantly sorry that she'd responded so tersely. If she continued in this vein, he'd demand an explanation, and she wasn't ready to talk about the sadness he'd detected.

"Are you really tired, or is something eating you?" he demanded.

Yes! I love you, but you don't want me to be the mother of your children. What an off-the-wall statement that would have been, she thought. Closing her eyes, she leaned her head on the back of the seat and sighed long and audibly, "I'm really that tired, Brian," she said, inwardly surprised at the truth in her statement.

"You're sure that's it?"

"I'm sure."

"Then settle back and take a nap. We've got another half-hour or so before we reach your apartment."

Pretending to agree with Brian's advice, Beth nodded. Keeping her eyes closed, she concentrated on breathing slowly and evenly as if she were actually sleeping. She wished her brain would shut down, protecting her from the implications she was reading into Brian's actions. Instead, for the half-hour trip, she wrestled with every course she could possibly take in dealing with their affair.

The options were few. She could break it off this very night. She could accept it as it was, let it play out its natural course and hope the parting would be mutual and amicable. She could continue as she was, praying that eventually her love would be returned. Finally, she could stall and evade.

By the time they'd reached her apartment, Beth had chosen the only option she felt capable of instituting. She stalled. Accusing herself of cowardice, she forced herself to give a lukewarm response when Brian pulled her into his arms and kissed her. Instead of melting against him, returning passion with passion, she leaned limply against him and remained as passive as she could. As soon as he lifted his mouth from hers, she yawned.

"I hope that yawn means you're tired," Brian commented, loosening his hold on her and rubbing his palms in soothing circles over her back. "I don't think my ego could stand my boring you."

Avoiding his eyes, Beth nestled her head into the crook of his shoulder. "Never boredom," she stated sleepily, breathing in the scent of him and luxuriating in the feel of his body. Boring? Never. Even before Brian had awakened to her, he'd been interesting, and once he'd returned to function, he'd become the most exciting man she'd ever known. She couldn't imagine being bored even if she spent the next fifty years listening to Brian read the telephone book!

Brushing his lips against her forehead, he murmured, "Just as well, I suppose. I've got a six o'clock flight to catch to Atlanta tomorrow morning."

Setting her away from him, he rested his hands on her waist and told her about his trip. Minutes later, he'd given her one more short kiss and instructions to rest up while he was gone.

Beth slumped against the wall and stared at the closed door. Five days. She had five days without the distraction of his presence in which to reach some sort of decision.

BETH CAME AWAKE slowly, savoring the delicious feeling of being cradled in Brian's arms. "Mmmmm..." she moaned softly, snuggling back down into the warmth of the bed and the pleasure of her dream. Brian's arm was draped around her waist. His long body was curled around hers. His lips were brushing against the curve of her shoulder. If only she didn't have to wake up and go to work.

Reluctantly she opened one eye and directed her gaze toward the clock perched on her nightstand. It wasn't there. Frowning, she squeezed her eyes shut, then opened them again. No alarm clock and the wrong nightstand!

This was no dream. She *was* in Brian's bed, and judging by the amount of light streaming through the windows it was well into the morning.

"Oh, no!" She jerked upright, flung the covers aside and bolted off the mattress.

"Wh...what the...?" Startled out of his own dreams by an abrupt draft of cold air, Brian rolled to a sitting position. Yawning and rubbing the sleep from his eyes, he watched in silent fascination as a delightfully naked Beth tore around the room.

"I'll never get to work on time." She grabbed up her panties and slipped them on. "I never should have fallen asleep." Dropping to her hands and knees, she groped under the bed in search of her bra. She came up empty-handed.

Rocking back on her heels, she surveyed the floor, spied her slacks and one shoe. As if she thought they would run away, she pounced on them. "At least I'm making progress," she muttered as she limped around the room looking for the rest of her clothing. "I knew it. I knew this was going to happen one of these nights." Nude to the waist, hands on hips, she swept the room with a searching glare.

Why last night, of all nights, had they flung their clothes everywhere in a wild frenzy before making wild, glorious love? Because Brian had been out of town for most of the week, and as soon as she saw him, all her fine speeches had gone out the window. She simply had to face the fact that she had no resistance to the man. Recalling their reunion at the airport, she figured they'd been lucky to make it back to his apartment.

Considering what had happened on the way up to the penthouse, she'd count herself luckier still if none of her clothes had spent the night in the elevator. She could only hope she'd find enough of them inside the apartment to enable her to drive home looking relatively decent. That might not have been too risky if it had been the middle of the night, but the sun was shining brightly. She supposed she could borrow a shirt from

Brian, but she didn't relish driving with only one shoe; with the earnest onset of autumn, it was too cold to be running around barefoot.

Ever since he'd stormed into her apartment the night after the infamous massage, most nights had ended in one or the other of their apartments. At some point in the wee hours, one of them always had to get up, dress and return home. Last night, the law of averages had finally caught up with them; after making love, they'd fallen into an exhausted sleep.

"This what you're looking for?" Brian asked, dangling a scrap of lace and lycra from one extended finger.

"Oh, good, you found it." Reaching out, Beth sent him a faint smile of relief. "Toss it over here."

Brian grinned devilishly and continued to twirl the bra around his finger. "Come and get it," he challenged, totally enthralled by the sway of her full breasts as she charged toward him.

"Give me that," she demanded impatiently, making a wild swipe for her bra.

But at the last second Brian jerked it out of reach. Losing her balance, Beth landed on his chest. Immediately he swept his arms around her and held her in place while he kissed her long and deep.

"Now that's the way to start the morning off right," he said against her throbbing lips several moments later. Beth wiggled against him, struggling to get up. Her bare breasts rubbed against his chest and Brian groaned. "Revise that. It's going to get even better."

He rolled with her until she was pinned beneath him. "I think this is where we left off when we took a break last night," he said, then nuzzled a path down her throat toward her quivering breasts.

"Brian..." she protested weakly as his tongue teased one rosy peak and then the other. She pushed against his shoulders. "Please stop. I have to go home, change and get to work. I'm going to be at least a half-hour late as it is."

"How about an hour late?" he suggested as he settled himself between her thighs. His hands fumbled at the hook and zipper of her slacks.

Beth pushed his hands away. "No!"

Responding to the determination in her voice, Brian let her go, albeit reluctantly. Beth slithered off the bed, snatched up her bra and continued her search for her missing shoe and sweater. In exasperation, she turned on Brian and scowled. "You could help me, you know."

"Try the hallway," he instructed. Leaning toward the edge of the bed, he peered beyond her. "I think I see a patch of green out there, maybe even a shoe."

"Why didn't you say so before?" Beth stomped out of the bedroom and recovered the missing articles, donning them as she moved through the apartment. She'd gathered her purse and had one hand on the doorknob before Brian caught up with her.

Flattening his nude body up against the solid slab of oak, he effectively blocked her exit. "Hold it. Aren't you even going to say goodbye?"

"Goodbye. Now let me go."

He didn't budge. "I don't remember your being so foul tempered in the morning. You used to come singing into the convalarium, so chipper I could barely stand you. What happened?"

"You never saw me when I was late. I hate being late. Now move out of the way."

He still didn't budge. Instead he folded his arms across his chest and planted himself more firmly in front of her. In spite of her irritation, Beth began to chuckle. "Do you know how ridiculous you look standing there without a stitch on?"

"You didn't find my body so ridiculous last night, my love," he reminded her with a leering grin.

A flush of red rose in her cheeks as she remembered all the things she'd done to him the night before. She'd worshipped every inch of him. "Brian, I really have to get going," she stated slowly and evenly, keeping her gaze directed at his face. "Don't you have to go to work today?"

"Yes, but I only have to ride the elevator down a few floors. I've got plenty of time. You'd have more time if you lived in this building. It's only a five-minute drive to the Shelton Center from here."

"I can't afford the rent."

"It could be free," he informed her in a slightly halting tone. His eyes penetrated her, reaching beyond the surface to her soul. "Come live with me and be my love."

Nonplussed, Beth stared wide-eyed and open-mouthed at him. What was he asking?

With the tip of his finger, Brian nudged her chin and closed her mouth. "I'm serious, Beth. We've gone on this way long enough."

Watching his face come closer to hers until his features were a blur, Beth stood spellbound as he kissed her. His lips brushed hers lightly, then settled over her mouth so sweetly Beth could think of nothing but how much she loved this man. Did she want to live with him? Yes, she did. Did she want to be more than his live-in lover? The answer to that was yes, too.

She wanted both love and marriage, which was the only thing that stood in the way of her telling him she would gladly settle for less. Agreeing to live with him might satisfy him, but it would only make her yearn all the more for what was missing in their relationship—total commitment.

"Think about sleeping all night, every night, in my arms and waking up every morning to my kisses," he uttered tenderly, averting his face as he stepped away from the door.

Whatever his tone, Beth sensed he was delivering an ultimatum. That feeling was confirmed when he stated bluntly, "Don't answer me now. Go to work. But I'll be waiting for you and your decision here tonight."

That said, he pushed her through the doorway with a gentle but firm shove.

Throughout the day, Beth could think of nothing else but how marvelous it would be to sleep all night, every night, in Brian's arms and then wake up to his kisses. From the outset, she and Brian had made terrific lovers and their affair was as passionate now as it had been at the beginning. Nothing had changed there, and it looked as though they would continue to be content in that respect for as long as they stayed together.

As Brian had said, living together in the penthouse would be more convenient and practical for both of them. And he was right: they had gone on long enough under the present conditions. Logically, it was high time she did something to prevent a repeat of this morning's episode, something to simplify her schedule. As much as she wanted to avoid making such a decision, she had to choose between living with him or ending their affair before it became impossible for her to live without him.

She considered what it would be like for her as his live-in mistress and how the people she worked with, her family and his, would react to the news. All who loved her would support her choice, even if it went against their own codes of morality. She was certain her friends would be happy for her, and her parents would slowly accept the choice she had made. She had an idea that the Towerses would welcome her involvement in their son's life no matter what her role. Indeed, if she decided living with Brian was the correct thing for her to do, no one she knew would fault her.

So what was her problem?

By the end of the day, Beth was forced to admit that her dilemma was the same one she'd avoided facing the whole week he'd been gone. She had this silly, old-fashioned idea that a man and a woman who loved each other were supposed to get married. She didn't want to be Brian's woman of the moment, and after all they'd meant to each other, she felt he had some nerve suggesting she settle for such a paltry position in his life. So what if he had issued an ultimatum? Before the night was over, Brian would be the one who had to make a decision.

At two minutes before eight, Beth stood before the door to the penthouse, making last-minute adjustments in the feminine arsenal she'd chosen to wear for the most important confrontation of her life. Her dress was sleek iridescent white silk, a shimmer of sequins and pearl beading from plunging neckline to zigzag hem. Twin starbursts of crystal and pearl beckoned at her ears and a pearl pendant clasped in a diamond pavé nestled between her breasts. Her long legs were encased in gossamer hose. Her shoes were off-white with stiletto heels.

Hair swept up in a sleek French twist that showed off the slender line of her throat, a cashmere shawl draped over her shoulder, she looked regal, and had every intention of stating her demands in a speech worthy of royalty. If Brian didn't like what she was going to say, at least he'd know what he would be missing when she walked out of his life. On that less than uplifting thought, Beth took a deep breath and knocked on the door.

Inside the penthouse, Brian jumped at the sound. *Don't panic, Towers! This is only the most important moment in your life.* Closing his eyes, he counted to three in an attempt to get a grip on himself. As soon as he was certain he wasn't going to suffer a mental breakdown before reaching the door, he glanced around the room, making sure the setting was exactly right.

The lights were low. The stereo was playing soft, romantic music. A log was burning nicely in the fireplace. Champagne was cooling in the bucket near the couch, and two empty glasses waited on the glass coffee table. In the candlelit dining room, the table was set for the late-night supper they would have if all went well.

As for himself, he felt every inch the nervous bachelor preparing to go down on his knees in hopes of getting a yes from his lady love. He knew he looked good in his black dinner jacket, dress trousers and white pleated shirt, but the silk bow tie was choking him. Knowing Beth liked the scent, he reeked of Kouros. Wanting so badly to impress her, he was going into this thing quaking like a kid on his first date. No matter what he did, he couldn't stop his hands from shaking.

A second, more persistent summons sounded at the door, and Brian knew he couldn't stall any longer. Wiping his sweaty palms on his trousers, he walked to the door, opened it, then gasped for air upon seeing the woman who stood on his threshold. He wanted to kick himself when the only thing he could think of to say was a stilted "Glad you could make it. Won't you come in?"

Beth's brows went up at the formal tone Brian had evidently decided to adopt for the evening. Maybe he thought their words should match the clothes they were wearing, she speculated, still recovering from the sight of him. He was so devastatingly handsome in his evening clothes she felt faint.

On further consideration, taking in the seductive setting he'd prepared for them, she felt more like screaming. How was she supposed to tell him that she didn't want him unless marriage was part of the offer, when in truth she would have wanted him on any terms he cared to make? If she spent more than a minute on that couch with him, listening to romantic music and drinking champagne, she'd be fighting a losing battle, and she knew it.

She had no choice but to state her business and take the consequences before she no longer cared what her business was. Walking to the other side of the room, she stood looking out the windows. With her back to him, she spoke very slowly and clearly. "Brian, I won't live with you. I just can't do it."

Beth held her breath in a silence that grew louder and louder with every word Brian did not say. Turning around to face him was the hardest thing she had ever done, but she forced herself. As soon as she saw his face, she knew he was so angry he *couldn't* speak.

Never had she seen a more livid expression on any man's face. But then she saw something else. She saw pain—raw, gut-wrenching pain. The kind of agony he'd displayed to her only once before. That time, in her anxiety to comfort him, they'd become lovers. This time she couldn't afford to do that, even though she loved him even more now than she had then.

"I'm sorry, Brian." Sweeping her arm to indicate the sensual ambience of the room, she continued weakly, "I know you were expecting a different answer, but that's the way I feel. It's over."

Brian reached out for the back of the couch and used it as a prop as he made his way around it. If he didn't sit down, he was going to fall down; he didn't want her to see how completely she'd just destroyed him. She'd spoken with utter conviction and he knew without asking that she wouldn't change her mind. She didn't love him—at least not enough to marry him. Now, because he'd delivered that foolish, ill-timed ultimatum, she wouldn't even continue being his lover.

Beth remained where she was standing in front of the windows. Brian sank down on the couch. His brain refused to function on any level but the one capable of silently reciting the painful words over and over. *She's leaving me. She's leaving me again. How will I stand it? How will I live without her?*

Beth eyed him for several moments, waiting for him to say something, anything. Then she realized he was doing what he always did when he didn't want to face what was happening to him. He had shut down. Eyes closed, barely breathing, he'd gone into himself. Every other time he'd used this means of escape, Beth had sympathized, but now it made her angry . . . furious . . . volcanic.

She marched over to the couch and stood over him, her limbs shaking with the rise of her temper. Gratified, she watched his eyes fly open as soon as she shouted, "Is your ego so fragile you have to shut down just because I'm saying a few things you'd rather not hear? Are you still that immature?"

Aware that she was attacking him in an area where he felt most vulnerable, Beth was astonished when he didn't respond by launching a passionate counterattack. Although his blue eyes burned holes right through her, his voice was emotionless when he spoke. "By all means, Beth, feel free to sit down and say all these things I'd rather not hear. You might as well end our relationship the same way it began—with you telling me how I should feel."

Pride forbade her not to react any more violently to his insult than he had to hers. "All right," she agreed tightly, and sat down on the white-cushioned chair opposite the couch. "But for once I'm going to concentrate on my feelings, not yours."

Between clenched teeth, Brian promised sarcastically, "You have my undivided attention."

As soon as he spoke, Beth launched herself out of the chair. She no longer cared about maintaining her dignity. The only thing she cared about was letting him know exactly where she stood. "After all we've been through together, asking me to live with you is the most insulting thing you could have done!"

"Insulting?" Brian asked before she could continue. "Well, that tells me something about your feelings, doesn't it? You don't mind going to bed with me occasionally, but look out if I make any serious demands on your time. Perhaps I'm the one who should be insulted if all you see me as is a stud service. I suppose I should be grateful you're telling me this now, before I could make an even bigger fool of myself."

"If you really believe what you just said, then you're already the biggest fool I've ever met!"

"And what does that make you?" Brian inquired caustically.

Growing more and more incensed each time he lashed out at her, Beth retorted, "I love you, have loved you from the first, and all you wanted was a mistress with magic fingers!"

Pacing back and forth across the carpeting, she pointed an accusing finger at him. "I thought we were friends and lovers, too. And I wanted to be even more to you. I wanted to be your wife, bear your children and share your life, not be a live-in masseuse who hops into bed whenever you snap your fingers."

Beth saw Brian's blank stare and realized he would never understand or accept what she was trying to say, not in a million years. "Well...well...as wonderful as we are together, I'm not hopping into your bed one more time, Brian Towers! I might love you until the end of my days, but I won't go against my own principles any longer. If you don't want to marry me, your days of therapy are over!"

Without looking at him again, she went back to the couch, picked up her shawl and purse, then headed for the door in what she hoped appeared to be a grand exit. Not for anything did she want Brian to see how close she was to breaking down and begging him to let her stay under any conditions he stated.

Hand on the doorknob, Beth was close to escaping, when she was snatched off her feet from behind. Too overwrought to scream, her surprise turned swiftly to outrage as she was crushed against Brian's powerful chest and swung around and around in circles. And he was laughing! After she'd bared her soul to him, the despicable man was laughing at her!

Before Beth could manage a single word, Brian planted a wet kiss on her startled mouth. She was too stunned to speak as he strode back to the couch and sat down with her cradled on his lap. Staring into his beautiful blue eyes, she saw her own feelings reflected there and gasped, "You do love me."

"Of course I do," he agreed joyfully. "I never stopped loving you, Beth, even though I did my damnedest to enjoy all that freedom you thought I deserved. After you left me, I got my degree as quickly as I could, then threw myself into work. I knew that you'd never believe my feelings for you hadn't changed until I saw and did everything you felt I'd missed out on in five years."

Feeling a surge of irrational jealousy, Beth wondered what role other women had played during that period. Besides encouraging him to complete his education and take up his position in the family business, she'd also urged him to get out and meet new people.

"I saw other women," he admitted honestly. "I even attempted to make love to one or two of them."

When Brian read her mind as easily as he had twelve months ago, she realized that he'd been hiding his true feelings from her for the same reason she had from him—self-protection.

He saw her slight wince and hastened to add, "But they weren't you, and I couldn't do it. It's you I want, Beth Crosby. Always have, always will. No matter where I go or what I do, that will never change.

"Even so, I didn't dare wear my heart on my sleeve and scare you off as I did before. Then you gave me reason to hope you might feel the same way. I wasn't hoping you'd agree to become my mistress, Beth, but my wife. That's why I got so angry when you threw my proposal back in my face. It seemed like a replay of the last time."

Beth couldn't help but believe him, for the truth of his statement was plain to see in his expression. Gazing into his adoring eyes, she read her own future. All the doubts and fears she'd experienced during the past weeks disappeared. She knew they were once again on the same wavelength when Brian closed his eyes, counted to ten and opened them again.

Recognizing the intimate signal that encompassed so many words, she whispered, "Do you love me, Brian?"

Blink. Blink.

"Are you going to marry me?"

Blink. Blink.

"Then let's stop all this needless chatter and get on with it."

Brian stood up from the couch with Beth in his arms, more than happy to comply with her wishes, but not until he'd directed a philosophical saying toward her. "It is a wise woman who knows when to shut her mouth."

"It is a wise man who knows the most pleasant way to shut her mouth."

Brian Towers was a very wise man.

Harlequin Temptation

COMING NEXT MONTH

Janet Dailey
Americana

Don't miss a single title from this great collection. The first eight titles have already been published. Complete and mail this coupon today to order books you may have missed.

Harlequin Reader Service

In U.S.A.
901 Fuhrmann Blvd.
P.O. Box 1397
Buffalo, N.Y. 14140

In Canada
P.O. Box 2800
Postal Station A
5170 Yonge Street
Willowdale, Ont. M2N 6J3

Please send me the following titles from the Janet Dailey Americana Collection. I am enclosing a check or money order for $2.75 for each book ordered, plus 75¢ for postage and handling.

_____	ALABAMA	Dangerous Masquerade
_____	ALASKA	Northern Magic
_____	ARIZONA	Sonora Sundown
_____	ARKANSAS	Valley of the Vapours
_____	CALIFORNIA	Fire and Ice
_____	COLORADO	After the Storm
_____	CONNECTICUT	Difficult Decision
_____	DELAWARE	The Matchmakers

Number of titles checked @ $2.75 each = $_____

N.Y. RESIDENTS ADD
   APPROPRIATE SALES TAX $_____

Postage and Handling $____.75____

               TOTAL $_____

I enclose _____

(Please send check or money order. We cannot be responsible for cash sent through the mail.)

PLEASE PRINT

NAME _____

ADDRESS _____

CITY _____

STATE/PROV. _____